A guy moved away from the crowd and walked toward us. He had piercing blue eyes. His black hair was combed back. In a tuxedo, he was totally hot.

My heart started pounding. My mouth went dry. My mind went blank.

"This is Ryan McKenna, my godson," Walter said. "Ryan, this is Lindsay, my soon-to-be step-daughter."

"Hi," Ryan said.

"Hello," I cleverly responded. Not.

Why did my brain go into total meltdown whenever a cute guy talked to me?

"Your cabins are right next door to each other," Walter said. "There's that little matter of you being too young to travel alone, so Ryan is there to look after you."

Great. Ryan, the hunk, was my baby-sitter.

CARIBBEAN CRUISING

Rachel Hawthorne

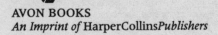

AVON BOOKS
An Imprint of HarperCollinsPublishers

Library of Congress Cataloging-in-Publication Data
Hawthorne, Rachel.
    Caribbean cruising / Rachel Hawthorne.— 1st Avon ed.
    p.   cm.
    Summary: On a Caribbean cruise, eighteen-year-old
Lindsay's to-do list includes having a one night stand,
but when her wealthy new stepfather introduces his
gorgeous godson as her traveling buddy, things become
complicated.
    ISBN 0-06-056507-1
    [1. Dating (Social customs)—Fiction. 2. Cruise
ships—Fiction. 3. Caribbean Area—Fiction.] I. Title.
PZ7.H31374Car 2004   2003021519
[Fic]—dc22   CIP
                                                 AC

First Avon edition, 2004
AVON TRADEMARK REG. U.S. PAT. OFF. AND IN OTHER COUNTRIES,
MARCA REGISTRADA, HECHO EN U.S.A.
❖
Visit us on the World Wide Web!
www.harperteen.com

FOR THERESA
THANKS FOR ALWAYS BEING THERE

CHAPTER 1

The Enchantment Night One

"I can't believe it! Everything is totally amazing!"

I couldn't believe it either as Julie Barnes and I gazed around one of the atriums of *The Enchantment*. The name suited this ship. I was definitely enchanted. It was huge and luxurious. I figured it would take all ten nights of the cruise simply to walk from one end of the ship to the other.

"Come on," I said, nudging Julie's arm. "Let's check out my cabin."

Julie was my best friend. Like me, she had blond hair. But her eyes were blue, while mine were green. And she was a little shorter than me, which meant she had a difficult time keeping pace when I was in a hurry like I was in now. I just wanted to see everything as quickly as possible. There was so much to take in. My time here would be short, and I didn't want to waste a single minute.

"Slow down, Lindsay," Julie ordered. "Your cabin's not going anywhere."

No, it wasn't, but I was anxious to see it, to get settled in. Still, I did slow down as we walked along a wide corridor, which closely resembled a boulevard. Stores and restaurants lined both sides. Plants, statuettes, artwork, festive lights, and a domed ceiling created an openness that I hadn't expected within a ship. It was like touring a gigantic mall—one of my favorite places to hang out. With so many people mingling around, it was like a bustling city floating on the ocean. I was a little overwhelmed by the crowds and the vastness of the ship.

"It's just not fair that I have to work and can't go on this cruise with you," Julie lamented.

Those words had become Julie's mantra ever since I'd told her that I was going on my trip.

"I'd give anything if you could come," I said. We'd shared everything since kindergarten. I couldn't imagine not sharing this too.

"I know. You have to send me a postcard from every port," she commanded.

"I will. I promise."

"And since you are so into making lists, I expect a report listing all the yummy details about every guy you meet."

I laughed. I was a little obsessed with lists. I

liked organization and had compiled several different lists as soon as I found out I was going on a cruise—everything I needed to buy before I came onboard, all the items I needed to pack, and everything I planned to do while I was on this cruise.

"Maybe I'll just send you a list of their names. I'm hoping there will be so many that I won't have room on the postcards to tell you about all of them."

"That's a definite possibility," she said. "Have you ever seen so many cuties in one place?"

"Nope." From the moment I'd checked in and we'd started our quick tour of the ship, I'd seen at least a dozen guys who I thought I'd like to get to know better. Each one was smiling, laughing, or talking with someone.

"I think it is so romantic that Walter is going to marry your mom on a cruise ship," Julie said.

"He's definitely gone all out."

Walter Hunt was quiet and reserved, but when he spoke, people listened and did as he asked. Mostly because his name appeared on a famous list of the top one hundred wealthiest people in the world.

Hence the cruise. A special honeymoon for

him and his new bride—who just happened to be my mom—and anyone else who wanted to tag along. Of which I was undeniably one.

They say that most people are introduced by a friend to the person they'll marry. That's how Mom met Walter. She was attending a friend's funeral. Her friend had worked for Walter's company so Walter had gone to the funeral as well. He and Mom met, hit it off, and now my life was on the verge of changing forever in ways that I'd never really anticipated. And truthfully, it's something I was having a hard time comprehending. For as long as I could remember, it had always been just me and Mom. Now it would be me, Mom, and Walter.

Still, Walter was nice and I liked him. I thought he'd be good for my mom. I was heading off to the University of Texas in the fall, and I'd been a little worried about Mom dealing with the empty nest. So I was definitely in favor of her marrying Walter.

And I was going to be a bridesmaid for the first time in my life. I had no doubt that I was embarking on a summer of firsts. And I planned for most of them to take place on this cruise.

I didn't think most cruise ships allowed wedding guests onboard, but Walter had made special arrangements so he and Mom could have their friends and family attend the wedding. He'd reserved the top deck for the ceremony. At midnight we'd have our official bon voyage and prepare to leave the port of Galveston. The guests would depart, and the ship would sail away into the night toward the Caribbean.

"I can't believe you are going to spend ten nights on this ship. Did you see all the stores we just passed on that boulevard?" Julie asked.

"I know. It's like a fancy mall or something. Plus there are lots of little shops on the islands. They're supposed to have some great bargains. Good thing I've been saving all my paychecks."

While Julie tore ticket stubs at our mall's movie theater, I worked in the concession stand. Sometimes I thought I'd never eat another bag of buttered popcorn in my entire life. Just the aroma of buttered popcorn made me lose my appetite.

Julie glanced over at me. "If you run out of money, I'm sure Wealthy Walter will buy you anything you want."

"Yeah, but I'm not totally cool with that," I confessed. "I mean I know he's marrying my mom, and after tonight, he'll be like . . . my dad, but I'm a little old to be needing a dad now."

My real dad had been killed in a car accident when I was three. I was too young to really have any memories of him, which makes me sad sometimes. I know it seems strange to miss someone I'd barely known, but I often did.

"I don't know why you're bothered about spending Walter's money," Julie said. "I'd spend it in a flash."

I couldn't explain the reason I wasn't comfortable asking Walter for money. He was paying for the cruise. He'd given me a special credit card to use whenever I purchased anything onboard the ship: food, drinks, souvenirs, whatever I wanted. He was paying the bill when the trip was over. Even though I knew he could afford it, I didn't want to take advantage of him.

Julie and I stepped onto the glass-enclosed elevator. Before the door closed, three guys about our age joined us. They grinned at us, we smiled at them. I punched the button for the floor—correction, for the deck—where my cabin was.

"The fancy deck," one of the guys said as he leaned over and punched a button for a deck two below mine. "First cruise?"

I cast a glance over at Julie, then nodded. "Yeah."

"Us too." He broadened his grin and winked. "So far, so good."

The elevator stopped. "See you around," he said as he and his friends got off.

As soon as the door closed, Julie squeezed my arm. "He was flirting with you!"

I shook my head. "No way! He was just being nice."

She groaned. "No, he wasn't. Lindsay, you should have given him your name, shown more interest. If you want this to be the best time ever, you've got to stop being so shy around guys."

"I will. As soon as we leave port," I insisted. I'd dated a few boys in high school, but I'd never been serious about anyone. I'd spent most of my time studying, and I'd been rewarded by graduating in the top of my class.

Julie, on the other hand, had always been comfortable around guys. Probably because she had three brothers. She also had a steady boyfriend—Ben.

I saw this cruise as my opportunity to break out of my shell, to meet guys and flirt and prepare myself for dating in college.

I wanted to go places I'd never gone. And I didn't simply mean traveling to islands. I wanted to explore all the different facets of myself . . . and boys. I wanted to cut loose and do things that I'd never done.

The cruise seemed the perfect place to try new things, because even if I made a fool of myself, I'd never see any of these people again so it didn't really matter if I made mistakes. I could be wild and crazy. I could be uninhibited, stretching the limits, taking chances, completing my list of firsts. And no one would know that wild and crazy wasn't the real Lindsay Darnell.

The elevator stopped. As I stepped out, I shifted my backpack on my shoulder and pulled one of my small wheeled suitcases behind me while Julie dragged the other along with her duffle bag.

With plans to meet up later, Mom and I had parted ways right after we came onboard and checked in. Mom and Walter were staying in a honeymoon suite. I had their cabin number and could find them if I needed to, but I certainly had no plans to go searching for them. It creeped me out a little to think of my mom on her honeymoon.

"It is too cool that you're going to have a

cabin all to yourself," Julie said. "You can do anything you want and your mom will never know!"

Those were my thoughts exactly. I had a feeling this new Cruising Lindsay was going to do some things that Mom definitely wouldn't approve of.

"I think Walter made special arrangements," I explained. More examples of his power to pull strings. From the research that I'd done on cruise ships, Walter and Mom were supposed to stay in a cabin beside mine since I was eighteen. Twenty-one was the magical age for solo cruising.

I wasn't really certain how Walter bypassed that totally old-school "not without adult supervision" restriction. He probably pulled some strings or something. For all I knew, he owned this cruise line. Whatever it was Walter did, I was glad he had done it.

Since Mom had always worked, I'd grown up fast and had acted responsibly for as long as I could remember. I never got into trouble, always did my homework, and as soon as I'd gotten a driver's license, I'd taken on a part-time job at the movie theater. So I really didn't think I needed anyone to watch over me on the cruise ship.

Walter apparently felt the same way. He had

managed to accomplish the impossible, and that was all that mattered to me. With the ship being as large as it was, once my obligations regarding tonight were over, I might never see Mom or Walter again. It was all going to be perfect. Except I did wish Julie was coming with me.

I reached the door to my cabin and pulled my keycard out of my pocket. I slipped it into the slot, cranked down the handle, and swung open the door.

My first thought was that I'd somehow mistakenly gotten the key to Mom's suite. My second thought was that Walter had spared no expense to see that I was comfortable. My cabin had a king-sized bed, a large sitting area, and an awesome ocean view. Or at least it would be, once we were surrounded by nothing but ocean.

I pulled my suitcase into the cabin. "Julie, is this cabin not absolutely incredible?"

"A small family could live in here," she said. "I thought rooms onboard ships were supposed to be tiny."

"I'm sure there are some tiny rooms somewhere," I admitted. "Mine simply isn't one of them."

"I bet this room cost a fortune."

"You know, Walter is more than money," I reminded her.

"I know, but geez, Lindsay, it's like you're moving into a totally different world."

I heard in her voice that she thought maybe it was a world away from her. As soon as we returned from the cruise, Mom and I would live at Walter's house. I'd have a big bedroom there too.

"You'll always be my best friend, Julie," I said softly.

"I know. I just wish I was going with you." She laughed. "I keep saying that, don't I?"

"Yeah, you do. And I keep saying that I wish you were coming too."

"But I'm not, and I need to accept that. Although I will totally take advantage of the few hours I'll be onboard. I'm going to hit the pool as soon as possible. Hey! Look at this! You've got a minibar. Can we have one of these tiny bottles of wine?"

"Sure. Have anything that you want. Drinking age is eighteen on the ship."

"Cool! What about gambling?"

"Nope. You have to be twenty-one to get into the casinos."

11

"That's weird—they'd lower the drinking age but not the gambling age?"

"Maybe they think kids will get into more trouble gambling than drinking." Although I didn't know if that was possible. It seemed to me that drinking was the more dangerous vice.

I shrugged off my backpack and walked across the cabin. I unlocked the glass door, slid it open, and stepped onto the balcony. I felt the breeze and smelled the ocean.

I glanced around. Apparently no one was above me. Around me all the cabins on this level had balconies, each separated from one another by a waist-high wall that offered a little privacy. I could sit out here with a good book and be alone in my little world.

No! I chastised myself. That's what I'd do if I were at home. Here, I needed to be hanging around the pool, meeting guys, being completely different from my normal boring self.

Julie joined me on the balcony.

"Is this not great?" I asked.

"Absolutely." Julie handed me a tiny bottle of wine. "I want to make a toast."

"There's probably glasses somewhere in there."

"Nah, this'll do," she said. She lifted her bottle. "Here's hoping you have the best time of your life!"

"I'll drink to that!"

I clinked my bottle against hers. This vacation was going to be perfect. I knew it without a doubt, because I was leaving nothing to chance. I'd made a list of all the things I needed to do in order to have a great time:

+ Soak up the rays.
+ Shop until I drop.
+ Drink margaritas by the pitcher.
+ Dance all night.
+ Climb a waterfall.
+ Snorkel.
+ Kiss a lot of cute guys.
+ Sleep with a guy for the first time.

CHAPTER 2

Leaving Julie at the pool, I headed for the ship's salon where Mom and I had agreed to meet. We were going all out: manicure, pedicure, facial, makeup, hair. Why not start the cruise being as beautiful as possible? Especially since tonight would be so momentous for Mom, and the start of an incredible adventure for me.

With my list of things to accomplish while I was on this cruise, I knew I was being ambitious by trying to cram a lot of excitement into a few days. But I just felt like this cruise was the chance of a lifetime, arriving at the most perfect moment. I'd just graduated from high school and closed the door on that part of life.

I was ready to open the door into womanhood. The last item on the list would help me achieve that—even though I knew that it would be the most difficult to accomplish. And I also realized that it could prove the most disappointing if I wasn't careful.

So although I was in a hurry, I wasn't in a rush.

I wasn't looking for someone to hook up with for all time. I wanted someone who would create fireworks the last night of the cruise, someone who would make this vacation one I would never forget. I didn't want to look back on this summer with regret or with a sense that I'd missed opportunities because I'd been hesitant to reach for what I wanted.

And I so wanted to no longer be a virgin. It was a rite of passage that was hanging over me, and I wanted it over and done with before I started college.

I spotted Mom and Walter standing outside one of the salons. Mom looked incredibly happy. She'd found her soul mate, her second love. My dad had been her first. But he'd been part of her life so long ago that I didn't at all resent that she was getting married again. I was truly glad for her.

Our eyes were the same shade of green, our hair the same light blond. Strawberry blond, Mom always said, because when the sun hit it just right a hint of red glimmered along the strands. Mom's hair was cropped short and curled around her face. I wore mine straight, past my shoulders. It had a lot of body, but very little curl.

When first meeting us people usually

thought that Mom was my older sister. She was very young when she married my dad. She had me a year later. It was kinda cool having such a hip Mom.

Walter was a bit older and very distinguished looking—dark hair with silvery wisps at his temples. Gray eyes. Every time I saw him, he was wearing a jacket or a blazer, like he always expected to meet someone important. Or maybe it was simply that he was important.

"Hey, kiddo," Walter said as I neared.

He was always calling me kiddo. At first I thought it was because he never could remember my name. But then I came to realize that it was his way of showing affection.

"Hey," I said. And it occurred to me that he might want me to start calling him Dad after tonight. I wasn't certain I'd feel comfortable doing that. I liked Walter, but I didn't really see him as my dad. I saw him as Mom's husband.

"Is your cabin satisfactory?" he asked.

I knew Walter wasn't asking simply to make small talk. If I wasn't happy, he'd do something about it. I couldn't imagine having as much influence as Walter did.

I nodded. "It's perfect. Thanks."

"Do you have any questions about the cruise, getting around, what to expect?" he asked.

"No, sir. I think I'm cool with everything. I studied all the brochures you gave Mom, so I know what I want to do." I wasn't going to tell Walter or Mom that I also wanted to do some things that weren't in the brochures.

"She's probably already created a checklist of everything she plans to do," Mom said with a loving smile. "Lindsay is a great believer in lists."

I was also a great believer in not sharing every list with my Mom. I loved her to death, but it's a fact of life that there are some things parents are better off not knowing. I figured she'd freak if she knew that I planned to have my own version of a honeymoon during this cruise.

"All righty, then, I'm going to leave you ladies to make yourselves more beautiful." Walter leaned over and kissed Mom on the cheek. "Although I don't see how that's a possibility."

I fought not to roll my eyes. As sweet as he was, sometimes Walter got a little corny, although I'm sure Mom saw him as being romantic. Come to think of it, I wouldn't mind having a guy tell me that I was beautiful.

"Have fun," Walter said.

"We will," Mom assured him.

As soon as Walter had disappeared amidst the throng of people, Mom hooked her arm through mine and marched me down the hall, like we were rejects from *The Wizard of Oz*.

"Are you sure your cabin's all right?" Mom asked.

"It's terrific, Mom."

"Are you going to be okay staying by yourself?"

"A little late to worry about that, isn't it?" I teased.

She laughed. "A mom always worries. I'm just sorry that Julie can't stay past tonight."

"Yeah, she's totally bummed now that she's had a chance to see a little of the ship. But I'll make friends. I'll be fine."

"Walter and I have a two-bedroom suite. You could stay in the other bedroom—"

"No way!" I cut her off. The last place I wanted to be was where Mom and good old Walter could keep an eye on me. As soon as my obligations regarding the wedding were over, I planned to hit my to do list with determination until every item on it was checked off.

"I love my cabin," I assured her. "I've been on my own forever. I love it."

"I know, but this is a little different. You'll be going places you haven't gone to before—"

"I'll find someone to hang around with. A lot of the activities are planned. I can hang out with a cruise director if nothing else."

"You're right. I need to get used to the fact that you're almost a young woman," she said wistfully.

And before this cruise was over I planned to cross the threshold into complete womanhood.

I followed Mom into the salon. It was way upscale. Nothing like the Cut 'n' Curl where I usually got my hair done.

We planned for this time to be our last afternoon together as mother and daughter before Walter came into our lives on a permanent basis.

Mom and I had a wonderful afternoon of bonding. While we had our facial, manicure, and pedicure, we talked about old times and how our lives were about to change.

Mom, being typical Mom, wanted to reassure me that our relationship would never change.

But I knew it would. It was changing now,

before our very eyes, as our makeup was applied by professionals and our hair was moussed and spritzed and twisted and curled.

The changes weren't so much brought about by Mom getting married as they were by me getting out on my own. No curfew. No having to account for my whereabouts.

Mom might believe that things wouldn't change.

But I knew differently.

I knew that they've already begun.

CHAPTER 3

After my French manicure dried, I gave Mom a quick kiss on the cheek and promised to meet her on the top deck a little before eight. Then I returned to my cabin where Julie was sitting on the balcony.

"How was the pool?" I asked.

"Awesome." She glanced over her shoulder, and her eyes widened. "Wow! You look more beautiful than you did prom night."

We'd both done the glamour thing for prom night. As a matter of fact we'd done so many things together that Mom was always teasing that we were like Siamese twins joined at the hip. That made going on this cruise without Julie seem like it had the potential of being a lonesome idea.

I mean, I'd taken vacations before—a few where Julie hadn't come along. But I'd always been with Mom. This would be my first one where I would be completely and totally on my own.

"Is your mom nervous?" Julie asked.

I sat on a deck chair. "A little I think."

I wanted to remain patient, not rush through one of the most important evenings of my mom's life. But I was also ready to begin my best summer ever, my best vacation ever, and I couldn't do that until after the ceremony.

Midnight was the witching hour. My obligations to Mom and Walter would be over, and I would truly be on my own, with my list in hand.

In the distance the sun was only just beginning to set, painting the sky in oranges, pinks, and lavenders. The water became a rich blue.

"You are going to have the best time," Julie said.

"I'm counting on it."

She held up a hand. "Don't tell Ben, okay? But I met at least half a dozen guys at the pool."

Ben was one of the reasons that Julie wasn't coming with me. She didn't want to be away from him. And he didn't want her to be away from him. Part of me thought it was wonderful to have that kind of commitment with someone—where you wanted to be with that someone all the time. But part of me also thought it was a little confining.

Maybe that was also one of the reasons that

I'd never gotten serious with a guy—because while I longed to have a relationship, I also wanted freedom to do as I wanted.

"Were they cute?" I asked.

"Every one of them was too hot to believe."

My excitement level soared at the prospect of meeting several cute guys. "I can hardly wait for this cruise to get underway," I told her.

"You are so going to have a blast."

"Ya think?"

"Definitely."

I smiled at her assurance and enthusiasm. It was contagious.

"Well, I suppose I need to start getting dressed," I said.

Julie was already in her dress. I figured she'd changed after she returned from the pool.

I went back into the cabin. Since my hair and makeup were already done, it didn't take me long to finish getting ready. My shimmering lavender gown was sleek with flowing lines, had spaghetti straps, and a gathering of folds across the bodice that dipped down and moved fluidly when I did. I loved it.

I put on low-heeled lavender sandals; a pearl teardrop earrings and necklace set. I wanted to look elegant tonight—for Mom. After tonight I planned to go totally casual. I didn't see myself putting on a fancy dress again until long after we'd returned to this port.

I held out my arms and twirled slowly. "What do you think?"

"Better than prom night."

"Anything would be better than prom night."

That was the night that I realized the guy who'd taken me wasn't destined to be a long-term part of my life. He'd been more into hanging around with his buds than dancing with me.

I grabbed my small white beaded purse. "Ready?"

"As I'll ever be."

We headed for the door.

"Where's your duffle bag?" I asked.

"I took it to the car earlier. I figured things would be crazy after the wedding and reception. Besides, I was afraid the temptation to stow away would be too great."

"I wonder what would happen if you did."

"I'd lose my job and possibly my boyfriend."

"Ben's not that jealous," I said.

"Yeah, right. I'm sure he'd absolutely understand my running loose on a cruise ship with a lot of hot single guys onboard."

Hot single guys. I couldn't wait to be let loose among them.

We left my cabin and walked to the elevator.

"There are probably just as many single girls on the ship," I said.

Julie shrugged. "I didn't see many at the pool."

"I'm sure not everyone is onboard yet. We don't sail for a few more hours."

The elevator arrived and we got inside. I pushed the button for the Starlight deck, where tonight's activities would take place. The captain was going to officiate the ceremony, which I thought was cool.

The elevator came to a stop. Julie and I stepped out onto the Starlight deck. It was so romantic. The sun was setting and twilight was easing in. Tiny white lights were strung along the railing. White cloth–covered tables had been set on one side of the deck. Candles flickered inside hurricane lamps. An ice sculpture of a mermaid wearing a wedding veil sat in the center of the table where punch cascaded into a bowl. Nearby was a multitiered wedding cake, topped with the traditional bride and groom figurines.

On the far side of the deck was a white latticed archway with flowers and lights woven through it. I could see a man wearing a captain's uniform talking with Walter. Chairs had been positioned behind the archway. People were already sitting in many of them.

Near the archway was a small orchestra. I assumed they'd play *Here Comes the Bride* and provide music for the dancing after the ceremony.

"Where's your mom?" Julie asked.

"I'm sure she's around here somewhere. We'll ask Walter."

He was walking toward us. Quite a crowd had already assembled. Many people were standing and mingling.

"Hey, kiddo," Walter said.

He really looked quite handsome all decked out in his tuxedo.

"Hi, Walter. You remember my friend, Julie, don't you?" I asked, tilting my head toward Julie.

"Sure do. Did you change your mind about joining us?" Walter asked.

"I changed my mind, but my bank account didn't."

"Maybe you can join us on the next cruise," he said. "They're addictive." He turned to me. "Are you ready for the big moment?"

"You bet."

"They've got your mom hidden off in a corner somewhere, but I wanted to introduce you to the best man before we got started here. I didn't think you'd want to walk back down the aisle with a man old enough to be your father, so I asked my godson to stand as my best man."

"Oh, Walter, you didn't have to do that." It seemed to me that he should have had his best friend, or whoever he wanted to stand with him, not make his decisions based on what he thought was best for me.

"Nonsense. Besides, he was glad to have the opportunity to come on this cruise, and it'll give you someone to pal around with since your friends couldn't join you." He glanced over his shoulder toward a group of people and motioned with his hand. "Ryan, can you come here for a minute?"

A guy moved away from the crowd and walked toward us, from the shadows into the light. He had piercing blue eyes. His black hair was combed back. In a tuxedo, he was totally hot.

My heart started pounding. My mouth went dry. My mind went blank.

"This is Ryan McKenna, my godson," Walter

said. "Ryan, this is Lindsay, my soon-to-be step-daughter, and her friend, Julie."

"Hi," Ryan said.

"Hello," I cleverly responded. Not.

"It's great to meet you, Ryan," Julie said.

It was great to meet him. Why was I shy about saying so? I wondered. Why did my brain go into total meltdown whenever a cute guy talked to me?

"His father and I go way back. Business partners in fact. His dad is holding down the fort while I'm away," Walter explained.

"That's nice," I said. *Lame, Lindsay, so lame.*

"Your cabins are right next door to each other," Walter said. He leaned toward me, an apology in his eyes. "There's that little matter of you being too young to travel alone, so Ryan is there to look after you."

Great. Ryan, the hunk, was supposed to be my baby-sitter when I so did not need nor want one. I absolutely wanted to die from mortification at the implication that I was too young to be without a chaperone.

"That's not really necessary—"

"I don't mind," Ryan interrupted me.

But I minded. I had my list of things to

accomplish, and I didn't need someone watching over me.

"Thanks, but—" I began.

"Mr. Hunt?"

The interruption came from a young woman wearing a ship's uniform.

"Yes, Cindy?" Walter said.

"We're ready to begin. If you and your best man want to join the captain beneath the archway, I'll get your bride."

"All right." Walter kissed me on the cheek. "See you in a bit."

Ryan followed Walter to the latticed arch.

"This cruise could not have gotten any better," Julie said.

"I don't know how you figure that."

"You've got that hottie right next door."

"Yeah, but he's Walter's godson."

"So?"

It was beyond explaining. Yes, he was hot. But I wanted wild nights, romance, drinking, kissing, and dancing.

I didn't want someone to "pal around" with. His presence was going to seriously limit my escapades.

CHAPTER 4

"**M**iss Darnell?"

I turned. Cindy stood there with an expectant look on her face.

"We're about to begin," she said. "If you'll come with me, I'll take you to where your mother is waiting."

"Right." Trying to stifle my disappointment that I wasn't going to be as "on my own" as I'd hoped, I looked at Julie. "I'll see you when this is over."

"Okay. I'm going to find my mom and sit down."

As I watched her walk away, my gaze shifted to Ryan, who was standing beneath the archway. He was definitely cute, and he seemed nice. Palling around with him would probably be fun, but it wouldn't help me accomplish the things on my list. I couldn't see myself being wild with someone I might see after the cruise, someone who was in tight with Walter. Very counterproductive.

It was a problem I'd have to deal with later,

though. Right now, it was time to get my mom married.

I followed Cindy to the rear of the deck where Mom was standing behind a little partition. She smiled at me with so much love in her eyes that it almost hurt to look at her. She looked really beautiful, and I knew I'd forever remember this moment with her. She was about to stroll off into her future, and I was waiting on the edge to walk off into mine.

"Here, I'll take your purse," Cindy said to me, and relieved me of my little beaded bag.

I hadn't really thought about how it would look to carry it up the aisle, or I would have given it to Julie before she walked away. Cindy handed Mom a large white rose-and-orchid bouquet, and gave me a similar but smaller one. The sweet fragrance wafted around me.

"Are you ladies ready?" Cindy asked.

Mom squeezed my hand and sighed deeply. "We're ready."

"I love you, Mom." I hugged her, and then followed Cindy out from behind the partition.

The wedding ceremony was a fairly simple affair, and I suppose that they performed so many on the ship that they didn't do rehearsals.

I was okay with that. I'd attended enough weddings that I had a good idea of what my role was: walk to the front, step to the side, and hold the bride's bouquet when the groom was ready to place the ring on her finger.

"When the music begins," Cindy said, "you'll simply walk up the aisle between the chairs and then take a step off to the side—about the distance that the best man is from the groom."

The best man. The cute best man. I wondered what he thought about me when we met. Probably not much. Maybe it was a good thing that Julie wasn't coming with me. She'd always been more outgoing than I was. Without her along, I'd be forced to be more assertive, meet people, and engage in witty dialogue. I wouldn't be able to sit back and let Julie take the lead. I'd have to be the one in control.

My mouth grew dry, my hands began to shake, and my knees weakened. Why I was suddenly so nervous was beyond me. It wasn't my wedding. I wasn't the one who was going to exchange vows. Yes, my life was about to change, but still, I knew I wasn't the one whom everyone would be gazing at. I would get a passing glance, and then everyone would start looking around me, trying to catch a glimpse of the bride.

At least that's what I did when I attended weddings. So I had no reason to be anxious about the next few minutes. They were totally my mom's.

The strains of *Here Comes the Bride* suddenly filled the air. I took a deep, calming breath. I could overcome this unexpected nervousness.

"All right," Cindy whispered. "That's your cue."

I walked up the aisle, trying not to look at the best man but finding myself looking at him anyway. He was incredibly hot. He certainly didn't look like a baby-sitter to me. Why did Walter think I needed looking after? And why was this guy so willing to do it?

I took my place, and turned so I was looking toward the rear of the deck where my mom was waiting. My heart tightened when the music deepened. Mom began strolling up the aisle. She wore a big, bright, glorious smile on her face. I hadn't expected to feel tears stinging my eyes, hadn't realized all the various emotions that would cascade through me at this moment: joy, loss, fear of leaving the familiar behind, apprehension of all that was going to change.

My mom was actually getting married. I felt as though the reality had only just now hit me. And it was quite a powerful blow.

Mom truly did look beautiful and happy. She smiled at me briefly, and then it was as though her whole focus, all her attention, settled on Walter as she came to stand beside him.

The captain's voice rang out, "We are all gathered here this evening . . ."

I slid my gaze over to Ryan. He was studying me, almost as intensely as I was studying him. I didn't think he was much older than I was. I found myself wondering if he had a girlfriend, if he had a list of things he wanted to accomplish on this cruise. Would he like the Lindsay who was standing before him now? Or would he prefer the one I planned to change into at midnight—the wild, carefree, always-having-a-great-time Lindsay?

Then I noticed that Mom was extending her bouquet toward me. Taking it from her I paid the wedding more attention as she and Walter exchanged their vows, their rings, and a kiss.

"Ladies and gentlemen," the captain announced, "I introduce to you, Mr. and

Mrs. Walter Hunt."

The music started up again. Mom and Walter began walking back down the aisle, and suddenly I was staring at an awkward moment. I wasn't exactly sure what I was supposed to do. Ryan stepped forward and extended his bent elbow.

I hooked my arm through his, and walked down the aisle with him.

"Your mom looked really pretty," he said.

I glanced up at him. "Thanks." And then I realized that was a silly thing to say. I didn't have anything to do with the way she looked.

"So you've known Walter a long time," I said.

He grinned. "Since I was born."

"I didn't know—"

"Oh, Lindsay."

Mom was hugging me before I realized we'd come to the end of the walkway. I hugged her back. Then I turned to Walter.

"Welcome to the family," I said quietly, just before I hugged him and kissed him on the cheek.

The guests began gathering around us, passing along to Mom and Walter their well wishes. Since this event was a little on the informal side,

I managed to slip away from the receiving line virtually unnoticed. It wasn't long before Julie joined me.

"Ryan didn't take his eyes off you the entire time," she whispered.

"Because Walter asked him to keep an eye on me."

She laughed. "No, silly. I think his interest is more than that."

I wondered if that was true. And if it was, what should I do about it? My plans for this cruise revolved around me having fun with people I'd never see again so I could be a little crazy. I would probably see Ryan again.

Waiters were walking around carrying trays with flutes of champagne on them. I didn't hesitate to take one when it was offered to me. Neither did Julie.

Walter caught my attention, and signaled for me to join him, Mom, and Ryan.

"I'll be back," I promised Julie.

I walked over to Mom. I was happy for her. I really was. But I was so ready for this wedding to be over so my real vacation could begin.

"Does everyone have a glass of champagne?" Walter asked.

There must have been almost a hundred people murmuring "yes" on the deck and nodding.

"Great!" Walter said. "Then I'd like to make a toast to the beautiful woman who changed my life, and her lovely daughter. Tonight I'm truly a lucky man."

He clinked his glass against Mom's, then mine, then Ryan's. Then Mom and I touched glasses. Then Ryan reached his glass toward mine. *Clink*.

I took my first sip of champagne. My lips kinda puckered and my tongue went up to the roof of my mouth.

"Wait a few bars, then you two join us," Walter said quietly.

Wait a few bars? What was he talking about?

Then I heard music. Older people's music. The kind Mom listened to in the car, and I would never program a button for on my radio. I wasn't familiar with the song that the band was playing. It certainly wasn't a song that I'd danced to at our prom.

People moved back as though an invisible hand had shoved them aside. Walter led Mom onto the empty space and began dancing with her.

Suddenly I realized what kind of bars Walter had been referring to. He expected Ryan and me to join him and Mom in the dance area.

"Let me know when you're ready," Ryan said.

"I'm not familiar with the music."

"Me either, but I figure we can fake it." He furrowed his brow. "You started to say something earlier."

I nodded. "Right. I didn't realize—"

"Ryan?"

Ryan looked over his shoulder. Walter was motioning us over.

"Guess that's his signal that we didn't start dancing when we were supposed to," Ryan said, taking my glass and setting it on a nearby table along with his.

Wrapping his hand around mine, he led me out to the dance area. Then he smoothly took me into his arms. I had my hands on his shoulders. His were on the small of my back. His lead—and the song's rhythm—was easy to follow.

I really enjoyed dancing with Ryan. We were completely in sync, and I loved the way he held me.

Ryan made a girl feel like dancing with her

38

was the only thing that he wanted to do. He had such intense, blue eyes. They gave the impression that he was giving his partner his total attention.

"All right," he said. "One more time. What were you going to say?"

I smiled, but it seemed so silly to say what I had wanted to. "I didn't realize Walter had made arrangements to have someone watch over me. I don't need a baby-sitter."

Ryan shrugged. "That's cool. I'm not really into baby-sitting."

I felt a sense of relief. "Good."

"So is your friend traveling with you?" he asked.

"My friend?"

"I think her name was Julie."

"No, like most of these people, she's just here for the ceremony."

"So you're traveling alone," he said.

"Right. And you?"

"Alone."

When the song ended I didn't know whether to be relieved or disappointed. I was a little of each I suppose. Especially when Ryan said, "Thanks for the dance."

And walked away.

But that's what I wanted. The freedom to be other than myself without anyone expecting a certain behavior from me. If Walter's godson was hanging around me, I'd have to be Lindsay the Dull, because our paths might pass in the future.

I went in search of Julie. I found her standing near the railing. A waiter walked by, and I snatched another flute of champagne off his tray.

"This could be the love boat," she whispered. "You and Ryan looked so good together."

"As we talked about you," I said.

"Talked about me? What did you say about me?"

"He wanted to know if you'd be on the cruise."

"He was probably trying to figure out if you'd be traveling alone."

I wondered if she was right. My conversation with Ryan *had* turned in that direction. She suddenly smiled brightly.

"Hi, Ryan."

I glanced over my shoulder. Ryan stood there, and he was holding another glass of champagne as well.

"You really don't have to watch out for

me, you know," I said.

A corner of his mouth hitched up. "I know. It's just that I think you're the only two up here who are under forty. Except for the staff, and I don't think they're allowed to mingle with the guests."

"Then you're welcome to hang around with us," I offered.

"Thanks."

"So your girlfriend couldn't come?" Julie asked.

I wanted to kick her. Ryan, however, seemed unperturbed by her pointed, nosy question.

"My girlfriend and I broke up in the spring," he said.

"Ouch," Julie said. "Break ups are hard."

Not that I would know. Sometimes I thought that I was the only person alive who'd never had her heart broken. I figured a broken heart symbolized that a person had first-hand knowledge of what it was to be in love. I'd yet to experience either of those rites of passage, so I could only imagine what Ryan had gone through when he'd broken up with his girlfriend. Julie knew because she'd once broken up with a guy and now she was in love with Ben. So she and Ryan were having a bonding moment here that left me feeling like an outsider.

"Ours wasn't too bad," he said. "We both realized it was time to move on."

Time to move on. That was how I felt. Like I needed to move beyond the innocence of high school and into the mature world of college.

"So are you in school or what?" Julie asked.

Honestly it was like she was Nancy Drew or something.

Ryan just grinned. "Junior. University of Texas."

Julie perked up. "Really? That's where Lindsay is going in the fall. She'll be a freshman."

"Cool. Have you decided on a major yet?" he asked me.

"I'm thinking computer science."

"That's a hard major."

"I know, but I took a couple of computer-science classes in high school and really enjoyed them." Programming was really nothing more than compiling lists of instructions for the computer to follow. And I was very good with lists.

"What's your major?" I asked.

"Biology."

I widened my eyes. "That doesn't sound any

easier than computer science."

"It's not, but I like it."

"What are you going to do with a biology degree?" Julie asked.

"I'm thinking sports medicine." He shrugged. "But who knows? I'll see how I feel when I'm finished. I'm trying to keep my options open."

"Do you live on campus?" I asked.

"I did, but next fall, I'm going to share an apartment with some friends."

"They're not on the cruise, are they?"

He shook his head. "No, they have to work."

"Bummer," Julie said. "That's why I'm not going on this cruise with Lindsay. Have you been on one before?"

"No. Walter has invited me several times. He's big into traveling on the ocean, but I've always had something else going on. This time I was free—and honored—that Walter asked me to be his best man. I've never been a best man before."

"I've never been a maid of honor," I said. "It was fun."

"I have a feeling the cruise will be even more fun," Ryan said. "Listen, they have a whole lot of food over there. I'm going to go get some. Can I get anyone anything?"

"No, thanks," I said.

Julie, much to my surprise, said the same thing. I figured she'd convince him to bring something back for me.

"All right, then," he said. "I'll catch up with you later."

As soon as he was out of hearing range, Julie said, "He is totally nice. You are going to have so much fun."

"Yeah, he is."

I knew she also thought that I was going to be having fun with Ryan. But I wasn't planning on it.

Ryan was nice, but he was Walter's godson and he goes to the same university I'm going to attend. So he was definitely not a candidate for my last-night fling. And I didn't figure another guy would show any interest in me if he thought I was with Ryan.

I faced the ocean and crossed my arms on the railing. The night breeze had picked up. Lights from the ship and Galveston glittered off the water and muted many of the stars. I could well imagine that tomorrow night, with nothing but the water surrounding us, the sky would be twinkling.

"I've never seen a falling star," I said quietly.

"I bet you'll see some tomorrow night when you're out on the ocean."

"I hope so." I looked over at my best friend in the whole world. "I'm sorry, Julie, if I was snappish when I thought you were playing matchmaker earlier. I just want this to be the very best vacation of my whole life."

"I don't see how it can be when I'm not with you," she teased.

"It will be hard," I agreed.

"At least you'll have Ryan—"

"I'm not planning to hang around with him, Julie," I interrupted.

"Are you nuts? Why not?"

"Because I have a list of things that I want to do on this cruise, and it would cramp my plans if I hung around with him."

"A list of things? Like what?"

"Snorkeling. Sunbathing. Hiking. All sorts of things."

"I don't see how Ryan would cramp any of those plans."

"He just would. Okay?" I didn't want to reveal that losing my virginity was also on that list. That's where having Ryan around *really* wouldn't work.

"Because he's not on your list?" Julie asked incredulously.

"In a way."

"Pencil him in," she demanded.

"Julie, I want to have a fling while I'm onboard."

"A fling?"

I nodded. "A summer fling. A cruise fling. One special night."

"But Ryan—"

"Ryan and I might cross paths at school or at some get-together with Walter. And it would be uncomfortable. So he is definitely out. It has to be someone I don't know and will never see again."

"A fling," she said. "That is so un-Lindsay."

"I know. And to have the kind of cruise that I want to have, I can't hang around with Ryan."

"I hope you know what you're doing."

So did I.

The ship's horn blasted. Crew members began informing all the guests that they needed to disembark.

I gave Julie a hug.

"Have a great time," she said.

"I will."

"Stay up here and wave to me," she ordered.

"Okay."

I watched her disappear into the crowd of guests. I walked over to the dock side of the ship.

I could see people wandering onto the pier. I didn't spot Julie, but it didn't really matter. She knew I was here. I knew she was there. I started frantically waving, as other people—both on the ship and on the dock—began doing the same.

Another sounding of the horn, and we were moving away from shore.

Moving away from everything I knew. Everything with which I was familiar.

Moving into uncharted territory.

Into the unknown.

CHAPTER 5

"**M**ore champagne?"

I looked to the side. Ryan stood beside me, holding two flutes of champagne. I took one. "Thanks."

Turning I leaned my back against the railing. It looked like maybe two dozen people remained onboard. The band was still playing, people were dancing, and the waiters were walking around offering champagne.

I took a sip of my drink. Was this my third or fourth glass? I couldn't remember.

"I've never had champagne before tonight," I said.

"This is very fine champagne," Ryan said. "See how tiny the bubbles are? The smaller the bubbles, the finer the champagne."

In the dim light, the bubbles weren't that easy to see. Still, I said, "That's fascinating."

"I'm a constant source of useless information."

"No, really," I said, placing my hand on his arm, surprised that I felt comfortable doing so. It had to be the champagne working its magic to help me relax. "It was fascinating information."

He grinned. "Well, I heard that when you go on a cruise alone, you're supposed to study up on the ports of call so you can be an informal tour guide. Apparently women gravitate toward knowledgeable men."

"Really?"

He shrugged. "That's what some 'guide to having the best cruise of your life' said. But I spent spring break at Padre Island, and I don't remember any babes trying to hook up with guys because they could ramble off facts. I figure a cruise isn't that much different from spring break."

"At least you have some spring-break experiences to compare this with. It's totally alien to me."

"You seem to be managing it all right so far. Want to dance again?"

I was suddenly feeling very adventuresome. And my wild and crazy cruise was supposed to be starting now anyway. Besides, as Julie had pointed out, Ryan was nice. I nodded. "Sure."

We danced until the lights from Galveston faded into the distance. Sometimes we drank champagne while we danced, and sometimes we simply danced. With the bubbly wine coursing through my system, the dim lights, and the soft music, the night felt almost magical.

I closed my eyes and almost fell asleep right there on Ryan's shoulder. I stumbled. He steadied me.

"I think you've had too much champagne," he said.

We were barely moving our feet. I didn't have the strength, and I certainly didn't mind if he didn't either.

"I think you're right. It's making me really sleepy."

"You don't think being sleepy has anything to do with it being almost two o'clock in the morning?"

I straightened. "Is it that late? I had no idea."

As I glanced around, everything seemed to spin. When had almost everyone left? Only Mom and Walter were still dancing, and like Ryan and me, they were barely moving.

"Is the party over?" I asked.

"Just about. Want me to walk you back to your cabin?"

I was feeling a little light-headed, a little

dizzy. I grinned at him. "Sure. I need to say good-bye to Mom first."

I walked over to Mom and tapped on her shoulder. She glanced over and stopped dancing. "Are you off to bed now?"

I nodded. "Yeah."

"All right. Don't forget about our dinner date tomorrow."

Mom wanted to touch base with me before we started hitting other ports and things got crazy. "I won't."

She hugged me. "Good night."

I waved at Walter. "Good night."

As we started to leave, Walter called after Ryan, "Take good care of my daughter now."

"I will," Ryan said.

I wanted to groan—at Walter's request and Ryan's response.

"I told you—" I began.

"I know," he cut in. "You don't need anyone watching out for you. Trust me. If I'd told Walter that, we'd still be explaining things to him. He's new at being a father, so he's probably going to be overprotective at first."

"I'm beginning to figure that out."

On our way toward the elevator, Ryan

grabbed a bottle of champagne out of a bucket of ice. "No sense in it going to waste," he said.

As we rode the elevator to our deck, I wondered who he planned to drink it with. Was he planning to share it with me? Should I invite him into my cabin? Should we extend the party?

The elevator stopped and we stepped out of the glass enclosure and into the hallway. The walls spun around me.

"Oh." I reached out and found Ryan's arm. I steadied myself.

"Woozy?" he asked.

"A little. I guess it was the elevator."

"Just hold onto my arm for support. It's not that far to our rooms."

"Aren't you dizzy?"

"Nope."

How many glasses had I had? I couldn't remember. "I've never had champagne before."

He laughed. It was a nice, deep rumble. "You've said that already."

"Oh, that's right. I forgot. Champagne seems to make me forget things." It even seemed to make me forget why I had reservations about spending time with Ryan. I remembered that I'd had concerns earlier, but now I couldn't remember what they were. They couldn't have been very important. Julie was right. He was hot, and he was fun to be with.

"I have a balcony," I said, feeling very happy, content, and a little giddy. "Want to see?"

I reached for my key—

And realized that I didn't have my purse. I quickly turned around to see where I'd dropped it. The walls, the ceiling, and the floor spun with me. I leaned back against the wall for support.

"Are you okay?" Ryan asked.

"I don't have my key."

"How can you not have your key?"

I shook my head. I was woozy, but I remembered . . . remembered giving my purse to Cindy right before the ceremony. Bummer. Total bummer.

"I gave my purse to Cindy. The cruise director or whatever she was. The one who was directing the wedding. Do you know if she's still up there?"

"I don't know. But I don't think you'll make it back to the top deck."

Unfortunately I didn't think I'd make it either. I wanted to curl up on my bed and go to sleep. Right now, even the floor was looking inviting. I didn't remember seeing Cindy when we left. What if she'd left for the night? I nodded. "You go look for Cindy. I'll wait."

"I can't leave you alone in the hallway. Come on. We'll go into my room and figure out what to do."

That sounded like a plan. Keeping my hand against the wall for balance, I followed him just a bit down the hallway to his room. Right next to mine. Just like Walter had said.

I couldn't determine why that struck me as funny. Everything seemed funny. The champagne was really getting to me, I guess. I was a little more tipsy than I realized.

He opened the door, walked in, and held it open. "Come on in."

I'd never been alone in a room with a guy before. My natural instinct was to stop at the door, but this was the start of the uninhibited Lindsay. I strode past him. "Oh, gosh, it's just like my room. And you have a balcony too."

I realized I sounded as though I was surprised, even though I'd seen his balcony while I'd been sitting on mine that afternoon. As a matter of fact, everything I said sounded as though I was surprised. It was the bubbly talking.

"Why don't you sit out there?" he suggested. "Some fresh air might help clear your head."

He slid the glass door aside, and I stepped through. "Oh, wow," I said as the breeze brushed by me. "You can see the lights on shore. They're dancing around. Aren't they pretty?"

"Lindsay, how much champagne did you have?" he asked.

"I didn't count." I sat on the chair, slipped off my sandals, and tucked my feet beneath me. Then I laughed. "Am I drunk?"

"I think so."

"But getting drunk on champagne wasn't on my list."

"Your list?" He sat in the chair beside mine.

"The list of everything I want to do while I'm on this cruise. Things I've never done before." I held up one hand and touched a finger with the other. "Have a margarita." I touched another finger. "Go snorkeling." Grinning I leaned toward him. "I can't tell you everything I want to do. Some of it is a secret."

"I'm going to call down to the main desk and see if they'll bring us a key to your room." He got up and went back into his cabin.

Getting to my feet I swayed and grabbed the

railing for support. I followed him into his room. He went around the bed and was reaching for the phone.

I walked unsteadily across the room and lay down on his bed. Just like mine, it was king-sized. "Ryan?"

He stopped moving and looked over his shoulder. "Yeah?"

"The room is spinning."

He stretched across the bed toward me. "Close your eyes."

"Everything is still spinning."

"Hold my hand." He wrapped his hand around mine, and I squeezed his.

"Never had champagne before." I thought I was speaking slowly but my words seemed to run together.

"I never would have guessed."

His voice sounded far away.

"Ryan, this is the last thing on my list."

"What is?"

As my eyes drifted closed, I murmured, "Sleeping with a guy."

CHAPTER 6

The Enchantment **Day Two**

The next morning was supposed to be the beginning of my very best vacation ever, but I woke up and wondered if it could kick off with a worse start. My memory was fuzzy. My head felt like it weighed about a hundred pounds. My body so did not want to move. I didn't have the key to my room. And I was sleeping with the best man—a guy I barely knew.

And to make matters even worse, I had a vague recollection of revealing some of the things I wanted to accomplish while I was on this cruise. I almost groaned aloud, but I was afraid that Ryan would wake up. And then what should I do?

Speak to him?

Good morning, Ryan.

Simply smile and shrug?

About last night . . .

Laugh?

I drank way too much champagne!

Look bored, get up, and leave without a

single word spoken?

It wasn't as though waking up in bed with a guy fell into my *"been there, done that"* experiences because I'd never been there, done that—until now.

Of course that was the very reason that the experience was written on my to do list. Although when I'd written "Sleep with a guy," keeping my clothes on wasn't exactly how I'd planned to do it. I decided I needed to be a little more specific with my list. But to do that, I needed to get to it, and that required getting into my room.

I slowly opened my eyes. The morning sun was easing through the parted drapes at the balcony doors. I could see Ryan more clearly. The way his eyelashes rested on his cheeks. The hint of a morning beard on his chin.

We were on our sides, facing each other. His arm was draped over my waist, its weight making it seem as though I belonged to him. The palm of my right hand was pressed . . . well, it was pressed against his chest and I could feel the steady pounding of his heart.

Even with a wrinkled tux on, a tie hanging loose around his neck, and a couple of buttons on his white shirt undone, Ryan looked hot. His black hair fell across his brow. I had to clench my hand to stop myself from reaching up to brush it back into place.

I found myself half wishing we weren't both lying here with all of our clothes on. But with Ryan, that scenario was a recipe for disaster. He was Walter's godson. And I was a little embarrassed by my virginal status.

I mean I was probably the last remaining virgin of my senior class.

Julie had confessed that her first time had been awkward, clumsy, and filled with . . . well, disappointment, maybe even a little regret. I wanted my first time to be totally different. A cruise ship seemed like a perfect place to experience a once-in-a-lifetime moment. All I needed to find was the perfect guy for one night.

If the experience turned out to be as wonderful as I hoped it would, it would be a memorable night to carry with me always. If it was awkward—well, I'd never have to face the guy again, so any embarrassment I might have felt would end when I stepped off the ship. The guy wouldn't be in my life to remind me of any blunders I made.

My plan made even more sense to me now that I was actually waking up in bed with a guy. I was definitely wishing I'd never see Ryan again.

Not that *that* was going to happen. Why did he have to be Walter's godson? Why did he have to go to the same university that I planned to attend? Why had I told him about my list, and why, oh, why, had I slept in his bed?

Holding my breath I pinched the cuff of his shirt and held his wrist up while I eased out from beneath his arm. Then I lowered his hand to the bed.

Slowly, slowly, slowly I made my way off the bed. I crept to the balcony, eased open the door, slipped outside, and picked up my sandals. I snuck back into his room and headed for the door. My gaze fell on his nightstand. My purse! What was my purse doing here?

Then I remembered. He was going to call the front desk. He must have located Cindy, or she'd brought it by . . . I shook my head. It didn't matter. My purse was here and with it came my key.

I tiptoed to the nightstand and gingerly lifted my purse, then crept to the doorway.

I glanced over my shoulder at the guy lying on the bed.

I felt a twinge of regret, disappointment, and sadness which I couldn't explain. Ryan was handsome and nice, but I did not want my summer fling to be with someone I might possibly see later on.

I opened the door and walked out. Once in the hallway I searched my purse, retrieved my key, and went into my cabin. It felt good to be in my own haven. I crossed the room to the table where I'd left my backpack. I retrieved my tiny notebook where I kept my lists and turned to the last list— the list of things I wanted to do on this cruise.

I needed to be a bit more specific. As soon as I'd corrected my list, I headed for the shower. It was time to begin my best summer ever.

+ Soak up the rays.
+ Shop until I drop.
+ Drink margaritas by the pitcher.
+ Dance all night.
+ Climb a waterfall.
+ Snorkel.
+ Kiss a lot of cute guys.

   Make love
+ ~~Sleep with a guy~~ for the first time.

CHAPTER 7

After slathering on suntan lotion, I settled back into the lounge chair beside one of three pools that dotted the ship. This one was for adults only, so I figured it would be quieter than the other two, which did allow children. It didn't have curling waterslides or resemble a water park in any way, and that's what I wanted right now. I had a slight headache behind my eyes—from lack of sleep and too much champagne.

I was trying to ignore the discomfort, which wasn't too easy to do. Although I was wearing my sunglasses, I could still see the sunlight glinting off the blue water. Water almost as blue as Ryan's eyes.

Don't think about him, I commanded myself.

I was beginning to regret sneaking out of his cabin because now I had to figure out what to say when I saw him again. I didn't understand why male-female relationships couldn't be easier. It had to be that Mars-Venus thing that I'd read about.

I told myself that I really didn't have anything to feel uncomfortable about. Obviously he'd seen me when I was at my silliest, but he'd been drinking too. So he might not even remember me jabbering about my list. We'd slept in the same bed for one night. Big deal.

Although Walter had invited him so I would have a pal, I figured that Ryan hanging around with me would seriously keep the other guys away. I would never accomplish my goal of losing my virginity while on this cruise. So I'd cut Ryan free, and now he could pursue his own interests.

I adjusted my wide-brimmed floppy hat so my eyes were more shaded. I was thinking that I might need to invest in some superpowerful sunglasses. I closed my eyes, and let the warmth of the sun relax me as the ship cruised through the waters toward the Caribbean.

I tried to block out the sound of other people coming to the pool. It had been pretty crowded when I arrived, but the cacophony of voices got louder as the minutes ticked by. We wouldn't reach our first port until sometime tomorrow. Today I suspected most people were simply checking out the ship.

The lounge chair beside mine squeaked as someone sat in it. Too delicate of a squeak to be a guy. That is, if squeaks can be classified as being delicate.

I heard the movements of someone getting situated. I smelled coconut-scented suntan lotion.

Definitely not a guy. Too bad.

"Sorry to bother you, but could you get my back?"

I opened my eyes. The girl sitting on the chair beside mine was holding a bottle toward me. She was deeply tanned already. Her dark hair was cut short and had bleached spikes.

She shook the bottle of lotion in front of me. "Do you mind? I know it's kind of an intrusion, but I have this skin cancer phobia."

I didn't think her phobia could be too great when her bathing suit left most of her skin exposed. She was practically overflowing out of the top of her bikini. I glanced down at my chest. I was tucked neatly into place. Overflowing wasn't an option for me.

I looked back at her. I would have thought someone with a phobia would have been all covered up. Still, I understood that when it came to getting lotion on your back, you had to take whatever help was available.

"No, I don't mind." I took the bottle and quickly applied the lotion. Her two-piece was much skimpier than mine. Just above one of the strings tying the bottom piece together at her hips was a small tattoo of a red rose. She had other tattoos—a dragon on her left shoulder, and what looked like a delicate bracelet drawn around her left wrist and ankle.

I didn't have any tattoos.

"Did getting the tattoos hurt?" I asked.

She looked over her shoulder at me. "Sure, but they're worth it. You should get one."

"I wouldn't know what to get."

"Something that reflects your personality."

I supposed I could start keeping a list as ideas came to me, until one felt right—a rose, a heart, a moon and stars. It wasn't a decision I could make quickly because once the tattoo was there, it stayed unless I did something drastic like having it surgically removed or redesigned into something else. No, I definitely didn't want to act hastily here.

"There you go." I handed her bottle of lotion back to her, and settled into my lounge chair.

"Thanks. I'm Brooke Hastings by the way."

"Lindsay Darnell."

"Is this your first cruise?"

"Yeah. Am I that obvious?"

She shrugged. "Not really. You're just so pale."

I glanced down at my legs, and then over at hers. She definitely spent a lot of time beneath the sun, skin cancer phobia or no.

"So why are you out here by yourself?" she asked.

"I'm an only child, and I didn't bring any friends along."

"So you're traveling with your parents?"

That made me sound like a child. "Not exactly. My mom got married onboard the ship last night."

"It wasn't the wedding that had the top deck reserved, and kept us in port until midnight, was it?"

"That's the one."

"Wow. Someone in your family must be related to the president or something."

"Or something. My new stepdad. He has influence." It was all that I wanted to say. I didn't want to brag about Walter.

"He must. He and your mom are going to

want some serious alone time."

"I'm counting on it." Mom and Walter spending more time together would give me more time to myself.

She laughed. "My parents are celebrating their twenty-fifth wedding anniversary. I can't believe they've been married for that long. I had to practically beg them to bring me along. I wasn't about to spend time at home when I could be on a cruise meeting loads of single guys."

"So you don't have a boyfriend?"

"We just broke up. He was great in the sack, but out of it he was a total loser. You know what I mean?"

Theoretically I did. But I wasn't going to admit that I'd never had "great in the sack," or anything in the sack for that matter. Some things you didn't share with total strangers.

"Absolutely," I said, hoping she would accept my answer and not prod me for details.

"Why are guys like that?" she asked. "Why can't they bring their bedroom personalities along with them when they get out of bed?"

I shrugged. "I haven't a clue."

And I really didn't. My sole experience with sleeping with a guy had been last night. And it certainly hadn't taught me anything. Except that guys snored.

"Don't you hate the way they hog the bed?"

Ryan hadn't exactly hogged the bed. He'd been snuggled up against me. It had actually been very nice. Caring. Protective. Comforting.

"I guess that's the reason they invented king-sized beds," I offered.

Not really an answer, Lindsay.

"You've got that right. Still, it's not much fun sleeping alone. I'm going to find someone to take my mind off him. Or someone*sssss*," she said, stressing the plural, and sounding a bit like a snake in the process.

"Good luck," I said.

"Have you got a boyfriend?" she asked.

"Nope."

"So you want to hang out together? Maybe we'll both find someone."

Hanging out with someone who wasn't Ryan had definite advantages. I wouldn't stick out like a lonely sore thumb. "Sure. You bet."

"We'll hit the first island, St. Thomas, tomorrow. I plan to shop until I drop."

The Virgin Islands. It seemed a little ironic to me that I was a virgin heading to the Virgin Islands, hoping that by the time I left the ship my status would be vastly different.

"They're supposed to have terrific jewelry," I offered.

"That's what I hear. I also hear that most of the singles onboard hang out at Cruisin'. Do you want to go tonight? Scope it out?"

Cruisin' was one of the clubs on the ship that catered to those between seventeen and twenty-four years old. I'd read about it in the brochure, but hadn't had a chance to check it out. "Sure, sounds like fun."

"Cool. There is nothing worse than hanging out at a singles place as a single."

"I thought that was the point."

"No way. You don't want to look desperate." She leaned toward me. "Even if you are."

Did I look desperate? She'd already guessed that this was my first cruise. The next thing I knew she'd be announcing that I was a virgin.

"I'm not—"

"Oh, hunk alert," Brooke interrupted before I could finish announcing that I wasn't desper-ate. Although in a manner of speaking, I suppose I was.

Smiling broadly she sat up a little straighter on her chair, and shook her chest so it jutted out a little farther. Apparently she wasn't waiting until tonight to reel in her first catch.

I had very little to jut out with. I was practically a plank of wood compared to her. I'd never been self-conscious about not being well-endowed, but sitting here next to Brooke I was beginning to seriously consider the benefits of implants.

I glanced in the direction she was looking, and my breath caught. Ryan was striding toward me, and he didn't look particularly happy.

He plopped down on the end of my lounge chair. His swim trunk–covered thigh was against my bare leg. His shirt was unbuttoned. Between his thumb and forefinger, right in front of my nose, he was dangling one of my earrings.

"Found this in my bed this morning after you left."

Having never been in a situation like this one, I may have overreacted. I snatched it away from him. "Thanks."

"No problem."

"Well, isn't this an interesting development," Brooke said. "Lindsay, I think you were holding out on me."

Ryan jerked his attention to her. "Who are you?"

"Lindsay's new best bud. And you are . . ."

She left the sentence dangling, almost like an invitation. I didn't want her to think that there was anything between me and Ryan, or that I'd been holding out on her.

"Ryan was the best man at my mother's wedding," I explained.

"If you're going to have a man, you want the best," Brooke said.

Ryan gave her a crooked grin. "That's me. The best."

"I'll just bet," she purred.

Not that I could blame her. Ryan was hot. And she wasn't connected to him through Walter. Besides, it was obvious that he wasn't interested in me. Sure he'd grinned at me a time or two last night, but nothing like the way he was grinning at Brooke right now.

I didn't appreciate their coming on to each other with me sitting right between them . . . and I was feeling a little left out.

"Thanks for returning my earring," I said, bringing everyone back to Ryan's original reason for stopping by.

"Not a problem."

He grinned, tugged on the brim of my floppy

71

hat, got up, and walked away. Just like that. Gone as abruptly as he'd arrived.

Leaving me even more irritated. Tugging on my hat was something a guy would do to his kid sister—to bug her. And his grin was nothing like the one he gave Brooke. The one he gave her sent signals—"Come over here, and I'll show you a good time" kind of signals.

"You slept with that hunk?" Brooke demanded to know.

I certainly didn't want to admit that all I'd done was *sleep* with Ryan. Not when Brooke knew all the ins and outs of guys' sleeping habits. So I fudged the truth a little.

"It's really not a big deal. It was just a one-night thing."

"So you're not going to hang out with him anymore?"

"No. It didn't work out."

"That's a surprise. He sure looked like he could show a girl a good time."

"When I met him I thought the same thing." I immediately felt guilty about what I'd said. Ryan *had* shown me a good time. He'd been attentive during the reception. He'd talked with me and danced with me. But he was just a little too close to Walter for comfort.

"I honor territoriality," Brooke said. "But if you're not interested in him . . ."

What? What was she going to do if I wasn't sleeping with him? Go after him herself?

"I'm not interested in him," I said, although the words didn't sound quite right. Under other circumstances if I weren't on a quest to lose my virginity with a guy I'd never see again, I might have been interested in him. No, I'd definitely be interested in him. "But I'd be uncomfortable—"

"If he and I became an item?" she finished. "That's cool. There are lots of other guys onboard, and it's fun to have someone to hang around with."

I was incredibly relieved to hear her say that. I really would feel more comfortable if Ryan wasn't with us, because he might feel obligated to do as Walter asked, and watch out for me. I so didn't want to be watched out for. I wanted to be wild and have some uninhibited fun.

"So do you have any plans for the day?" I asked.

Brooke smiled brightly. "I sure do. I plan to find some men to run their hands amok over my body. Want to join me?"

CHAPTER 8

It was called a "Four Hands Muscle Melt."

And it was absolutely divine: the most wonderful massage that I'd ever had.

All right. It was the first massage that I'd ever had. I couldn't believe that I hadn't included it on my list of things to experience while on this cruise.

Brooke had suggested we head to the spa for a little spoiling. So now I was wondering how I was going to possibly get off the table when my body felt fluid. The room had been dimly lit. Enya had echoed softly around me. And two masseurs had worked in tandem to melt every muscle I possessed.

Hence the title. Four Hands Muscle Melt.

When they were finished, the masseurs had left so I could prepare to leave. It took me several minutes to gather enough energy to roll off the table. I put on my bathing suit and the thick, downy robe that the spa provided.

I padded out of the room and to the bubbling aqua spa. Brooke was already there. I truly didn't know if I could endure being any more relaxed.

But I was willing to give it a go.

I slipped off the robe, draped it over a nearby chair, walked down the steps into the warm waters, and floated over to where Brooke was already sitting.

"I may stay here forever," she said quietly.

"It's definitely heavenly."

"The best way to prepare for dancing all night. And the best way to get into the mood to seduce."

Seduce? I suppose if I wanted a guy, that's the way I needed to think.

"I was thinking about getting my navel pierced," I admitted.

"Go for it. Guys like it."

"They do?"

"Oh, yeah. Get your tongue pierced while you're at it." She stuck hers out. I hadn't noticed before, but hers was definitely pierced. She had a little black stud in the center. "Guys love a pierced tongue."

"Didn't it hurt?"

"You bet. But it was worth it."

I was having a hard time thinking that it might be worth it. I'd seen a TV show where a guy got his tongue pierced. It looked seriously painful.

I shook my head. "Think I'll just do the navel."

"Whatever. We can probably find a place on St. Thomas to get it done. We'll get you a tattoo as well."

"I could maybe get a tattoo," I said hesitantly.

She angled her head slightly. "It should reveal the real Lindsay."

I thought of her dragon, and was so afraid she'd suggest a bunny rabbit for me. Something tame and lame.

"A butterfly, maybe," she said. "I sense that you're evolving."

"Wow! I'm impressed. This is definitely a summer of change for me."

She smiled as though very satisfied with herself.

The idea of getting a tattoo was intriguing. As long as it was little, and in no place too private where the tattoo artist got to see more of me than I wanted him to see. Maybe on my shoulder, or my hip, or—

"So what's up with Ryan?" she asked suddenly.

I snapped out of my thoughts about tattoos as if someone had just stuck a needle into me. "What do you mean?"

She turned in the water so she was facing me. "I mean you said he was the best man. Did you know him before the wedding?"

"No, I met him yesterday evening, right before the wedding."

"And you've already slept with him? You are a wild woman! My kinda girlfriend! We are so going to get along."

I knew that I really should have confessed that all I'd done was sleep, but what would it hurt to be thought of as being a little . . . wild?

After all, I had plans to be just that.

"Was he really good?" she asked.

Yeah, he'd let me sleep, hadn't pressured me into anything, but I didn't think that's what she meant.

"Sure, he was great."

Her brow furrowed. "So how come you blew him off when he came to the pool?"

Had I blown him off? I tried not to encourage him to hang around because he would seriously limit my flirting with other guys. Had I been rude?

"We don't have much in common," I said.

"If he does the horizontal dance well, what more do you need?"

She dipped under the water, and I wondered what I'd gotten myself into.

She came back up, and brushed her wet hair out of her eyes.

"It's cool if you want to be all mysterious about him," she said.

"It's not that. It's just—"

"That you don't trust me with your secrets."

"No, that's not it. He was great. There really isn't anything more than that to say."

Suddenly I wasn't nearly as relaxed as I had been. If I stayed much longer, I'd have to go get another massage. "I need to go."

"That's cool," she said. "Totally. I'll see you tonight."

"Right."

I made my way out of the pool, and slipped on the robe.

"Oh, wait!" Brooke called after me. She rolled her eyes. "I forgot that I have to eat dinner with my parents tonight. I know it's lame—"

"It's okay. My mom wants to check up on me too."

Brooke grinned. "Okay, then I'll hook up

with you at Cruisin' at eight."

"Great." I gave Brooke a little wave. "See you tonight."

This evening was going to be so much fun. I could hardly wait.

I walked through the spa area and into the fitness facility. It was an amazing place. Floor-to-ceiling windows revealed a panoramic view of the ocean. In a distant corner I could see a stack of yoga mats. I'd gotten into yoga my senior year. It helped me relax before exams. Not as much as a Four Hand Muscle Melt, but better than nothing. And I enjoyed walking on a treadmill, going nowhere. In this room, going nowhere would still be interesting.

I turned. The free weights were on this side of the room.

And so was Ryan.

He was in baggy shorts and a sleeveless tee that looked as though he'd melted his body down in order to pour himself into it. Wow! No wonder he looked so hot in a tux.

He sat on the end of a bench, his elbow on his thigh. Wearing gloves he was gripping a weight, lowering his arm, and curling it back up. Totally focused on the slow up-and-down movement.

I could leave, and he'd never know that I'd spotted him. But I was feeling a little guilty about brushing him off by the pool. He didn't have to bring me my earring.

If Brooke saw him, she'd probably hotfoot it right on over there, and start that irritating flirting. Maybe I should warn him . . .

I strolled over. Close up I could see the dampness of his shirt, the bunched muscles in his arms. Obviously this wasn't the first time that he'd used weights.

"Hey." *Great opening line, Lindsay.*

He did nothing more than lift his eyes. "Hey."

"You do this a lot?"

"Four times a week."

"I do yoga."

"Really."

He said it like a statement he didn't quite believe. Not a question.

"Really. It strengthens your body and mind."

"Your mind must have missed a few lessons."

"Excuse me?" I snapped. I was certainly seeing a side to him that I hadn't before. What did he mean by that comment?

"Why are you hooking up with Sally Sleaze?" he asked.

"Her name is Brooke, and she happens to be very nice."

"She seems a bit pushy."

"She's enthusiastic."

He released a breath, and lowered the weight to the ground. "If you say so."

I really didn't want to get into an argument about Brooke. I was looking forward to hanging around with her. She struck me as the kind of girl who drew guys in, and I figured I could benefit from her experience, and find the perfect guy to end the cruise with.

I took a step back. "Well, I just wanted to thank you for bringing me my earring."

"Not a problem. Why'd you leave without waking me this morning?"

I shrugged and admitted reluctantly, "I wasn't sure what to say when you woke up."

He grinned. "Good morning?"

I really wished he wouldn't look at me like that. It made me feel like such a fool for rushing off. But then everything about last night made me feel like a fool. I tried to think of something to say that would turn the conversation away from the fact that I'd spent the night in his bed. "It was nice of Walter to bring you along."

He repositioned himself, bent over, picked up the weight with his left hand, and started curling his forearm. "He and my dad have been business partners for years. Walter kind of adopted me, treated me like a son since he didn't have any kids of his own. So Dad stayed behind to manage the business, and I got to come on the cruise."

"Lots of pretty girls around."

He wiggled his brows. "So I noticed."

"Do you think Brooke is pretty?"

"She's all right."

"She thinks you're hot."

"What do you think?"

How did I end up here? Witty comeback, witty comeback. Where was it hiding?

"You're okay."

He gave me that crooked grin of his again. "Thanks. I'll try not to let my head swell with that heartfelt compliment." He stopped lifting weights suddenly. "You know, it's really hard for me to keep count of the reps when I'm talking."

"Oh, sorry." I backed up a step. "I have to go get ready for tonight anyway."

"See you later," he said.

Not if I saw him first.

I couldn't figure out why my tongue got all

tangled up and my heart beat so loudly that I could barely hear myself think whenever I got near the guy.

My best plan of action was to make sure that I no longer got within sight of him.

CHAPTER 9

The Eiffel Tower was an upscale, swank restaurant where I was having dinner with Mom, Walter, and Ryan. Cloth-covered tables with scented candles in their center. A man in a tuxedo played soft piano music. The waiters spoke quietly. Everything seemed hushed.

I looked around, but I didn't see Brooke anywhere so I figured she was meeting her parents at another restaurant. I was constantly amazed by all that this ship had to offer. It had everything I could think of, anything I could possibly ever need.

I was even fairly certain that the guy of my dreams was somewhere onboard, simply waiting for me to find him. And I was pretty sure that he wasn't the guy who was with me now. I should have expected Ryan to be here, but it still took me by surprise. I suppose I'd thought it would be like it always was: me and Mom. Only now there was Walter. And with Walter came Ryan.

Mom looked more than happy. She looked

joyous. She and Walter were smiling at each other so much that it made *my* jaws ache, and also made me wonder why they'd wanted to get together for dinner when it was so obvious that they only had eyes for each other.

Corny, I know, but that's how it really seemed.

But here I was, ordering food that I could barely pronounce, sitting beside a guy I'd spent the night with. I really hoped that subject didn't come up during dinner.

"How are you enjoying the cruise so far?" Walter asked, smiling.

"Fine," Ryan and I said at the same time.

"Ryan, did I tell you that Lindsay is going to the University of Texas in the fall?" Walter asked.

Ryan glanced over at me. "No, sir, but Lindsay mentioned it last night."

Walter looked at me now. "So that gives you something in common. And you're bound to run into each other—"

"It's a big campus," Ryan said. "I don't even run into my roommates."

"What have you done so far on the cruise?" Mom asked.

Slept with Ryan.

Wouldn't she love that?

I told her about meeting Brooke and spending the afternoon at the spa.

"I got a massage. It was called a Four Hands Muscle Melt. It was fabulous. If you can find the time, Mom, you should get one."

"That does sound wonderful," Mom said. "I think I'll try to book one in the morning."

"I want you two to have loads of fun while you're on this cruise," Walter said. He reached into his jacket pocket, and handed an envelope to Ryan. "I got you tickets to the show."

I leaned toward Ryan. "Which movie?"

Laughing, Ryan handed me a ticket. "Not a movie, but a dance show. Kinda like a cabaret."

I looked at the ticket. Eight o'clock tonight. That was not going to work.

I lifted my eyes to Walter. He was beaming like he'd just handed me a diamond. I knew he meant well, and I simply didn't have the heart to disappoint him.

"Thank you."

He reached over and patted my hand. "You're more than welcome. You're my daughter now, and anything you want is yours."

Dinner seemed to go on forever. Walter and

Ryan talked about the upcoming Tour de France. I spent my time reassuring Mom that I would be fine exploring the islands with Brooke, and that she really didn't need to worry about me anymore. After all, I was old enough to vote.

When we finally finished with dinner, Walter and Mom headed off in one direction. Ryan and I turned in the direction of our rooms.

"Come on and smile," Ryan urged. "Dinner wasn't *that* bad."

I held up the ticket that Walter had generously bought for me. "I had plans for tonight. Brooke and I were going to Cruisin'. I was supposed to meet her at eight."

Ryan snatched the ticket out of my hand. "I'll take care of it."

"What do you mean?"

"I'll trade them in for another night and time. Tomorrow night we'll be in St. Thomas. How about the night after?"

It seemed I was destined to keep changing my plans on this cruise, but I found it difficult to turn down Ryan's offer. I really felt like I owed it to Walter to go see the show. But I had worked myself up into looking forward to spending tonight at the nightclub.

"The night after tomorrow will be fine," I told him. "Do you think we could get an extra ticket for Brooke?"

"Your new best friend?"

I grinned. "Yeah."

"Sure. Shouldn't be a problem."

"Thanks, Ryan."

"I'd better go take care of these before tonight's show starts, or they might not exchange them. I'll see you later."

I watched him walk off, then made my way to my cabin. I'd dressed up a little for the fancy dinner, and I wanted to dress down just a bit for tonight. I slipped into a pair of comfortable jeans and a white blouse that laced up the front and had billowy sleeves. It had a medieval look about it that I just loved.

I sat down at the table and made some notations for the night.

+ Drink margaritas by the pitcher.
+ Dance all night.
+ Meet some guys.

I slipped the key to my room into my jeans' pocket, along with the credit card Walter had given me to use when purchasing items on the ship. I put my purse into the safe in my closet, then headed for the club. I was so glad that I'd met Brooke. Going by myself would have really made me look desperate.

And even though I was . . . I didn't want to look that way.

CHAPTER 10

Cruisin' was a happening place. Colored spotlights roamed over the dance floor. Even with all the lights flashing here and there, the place still seemed dark and mysterious.

It took me almost ten minutes of weaving through the crowd and peering around people to find Brooke. And then we had to yell in each other's ear to be heard.

"Hey!" I yelled.

"Hey! Let's find a table."

Her suggestion was easier said than done. We wended our way around full tables and standing people. I decided that next time it would be a good idea if we got here a little earlier.

We finally located an empty table at the back, not nearly as close to the action as I'd like to have been.

"Getting picked up is like real estate!" Brooke shouted. "Location, location, location. Keep your eyes open for a table opening up closer to the dance floor."

The waitress came over. Brooke and I each ordered a frozen daiquiri. It would be my first daiquiri that wasn't a virgin, which may be a mistake considering how I handle champagne. But it seemed a little too much to be a virgin, drinking a virgin daiquiri, and heading to the Virgin Islands. I could see some country singer turning my vacation into a twangy song.

As soon as the waitress brought the frozen concoction over and walked away, Brooke tapped her glass against mine.

"To good times and hot guys!"

"I'll drink to that."

I looked out over the dance floor.

A lot of people were dancing to the music provided by the live band. I saw immediately that dancing here was way different from dancing at the prom.

Here, no teacher was going to tap me on the shoulder for dancing too closely or too provocatively.

"Drink up!" Brooke shouted at me.

I dropped my gaze to her glass. Half empty.

Mine was one sip short of full.

I sucked through the straw . . . too much, too fast.

Brain freeze!

Oh! I pressed my hand to my head. When the pain eased, I was hot. I didn't know if it was because of the rum, or the crowds in the place. It was like there suddenly was no air.

The music stopped, and the abrupt silence was almost deafening. Then conversations started buzzing around us.

"We'll never meet anyone way over here," Brooke said. She tapped my arm. "Come on."

I grabbed my drink, and followed Brooke through the crowd as the music started up again. I wanted to be on the dance floor, to be having a good time.

Having never frequented bars or nightclubs, being surrounded by strangers was a little harder than I had expected it to be. I nearly bumped into Brooke before I realized that she'd come to an abrupt halt. I peered around her. A table. Three guys. No girls.

This scenario had promise.

I could see one guy's mouth moving, but it was impossible to hear any of the words he was speaking. Brooke nodded and smiled, so I nodded and smiled.

The next thing I knew the guys were shifting around the table, and two empty chairs appeared. Brooke dropped into one, so I dropped into the other.

When the song ended, we all made quick introductions: Cameron had blond spiked hair and a pierced ear; David had black hair and a goatee, very artsy-looking; Michael's hair was cropped so short that he looked almost bald in a Bruce Willis sort of way.

As I sat there, I was having a difficult time thinking of anything interesting to say. Another song was blasting over the speaker, but I couldn't blame it for my failure to communicate. I simply wasn't skilled at carrying on a conversation with guys I'd just met.

A couple of days earlier, Julie and I had taken a quiz that tested flirting styles. Answering all A's meant you were a vixen; all B's, mysterious; all C's, a comedian. I was all over the board, which obviously meant that I didn't *have* a flirting style. Maybe that was the reason that I had so little luck with guys.

Brooke, without a doubt, was a vixen. She kept touching her shoulder to David's like they were sharing a secret and were in danger of losing each other if they didn't keep in physical contact.

Mine was more along the lines of a I'll-give-you-a-stammering-reply-if-you-ask-me-a-direct-question style.

"Where are you from?" Cameron yelled in my ear.

I smiled. A question to which I knew the answer. "Dallas."

"We're from Oklahoma."

"Not much beach in Oklahoma." I thought that statement might fall under the comedic category.

He smiled. "None at all."

The music died. I expected everyone to start talking since we'd be able to actually hear one another, but no one said a word. As soon as the band started up again, Brooke and David headed to the dance floor. Michael got up and moved around so he was on the other side of me. I was sandwiched in between him and Cameron.

"Where are you from?" Michael asked.

I was beginning to think that all relationships began with that question. "Dallas."

"Oklahoma."

So these guys obviously had known one another before they came onboard the ship.

"So you and Brooke are friends?" Cameron asked.

"Actually we met this afternoon."

"So who are you on the cruise with?" Michael asked.

Admitting I was here with my mom sounded so lame. . . .

"I'm by myself."

"Really?"

"My graduation gift."

"From college?" Cameron asked.

I laughed—torn between offering the truth and another lie. I went with the truth. "High school."

"You look older than that," Cameron said.

"I'm old enough."

With a grin that made me think I'd moved into the vixen category, he took my hand. "Let's dance."

And that's how I ended up in the middle of the colored lights on the dance floor. Bumping and grinding. Having a blast.

Cameron's moves included quickly jabbing his fists at the floor, then at the ceiling. A quick spin. Jab down. Jab up. Spin. But he was obviously having fun with it, and I enjoyed dancing with him. . . . Until I spotted Ryan.

The red light moved over him, darkness; the blue light, darkness; the green light, darkness.

And the cycle started again.

Each passing light revealed him dancing with a girl in a way that would have a teacher up in arms, rushing across the dance floor, ruler in hand. Close. Sensual. Hot.

Not at all like the way he'd danced with me last night. It was obvious that if this girl went to his cabin, they were going to do a lot more than sleep.

"What's wrong?" someone shouted in my ear.

The someone was Cameron, his brow deeply furrowed. Only then did I realize that I was standing there like an idiot. The music thankfully stopped.

"I like to wind down before the song ends," I said.

He nodded like I was a genius. "Cool!"

Then Michael was standing beside us. "My turn," he announced.

I'd never been so popular, and it was a heady feeling. Two guys were interested in me. I would have thought they'd be fighting over Brooke, the vixen.

Maybe my flirting style was better than I thought it was.

The drumbeat lead into the next song, and Michael and I were . . . well, I was dancing. I wasn't quite sure what Michael was doing. He was all arms and legs, punching the air, kicking, and spinning around.

It didn't help that my gaze fell on Ryan who was still dancing close to his—whatever she was—looking in my direction, and obviously fighting to hold back his laughter.

Still, I admired Michael's enthusiasm, and while I didn't quite match it, I didn't think I danced too badly. Michael seemed to think sticking his tongue out added to his charisma as he rolled his shoulders toward me.

It occurred to me that maybe, like Brooke, he had a pierced tongue, and was trying to make sure that I knew it. But in the fluctuating gloom of the club, a pierced tongue wasn't readily visible unless the stud came with a blinking light.

When the song ended, I patted Michael's shoulder and decided that his enthusiasm needed to be spread around.

"Thanks. That was fun. I bet Brooke would enjoy dancing with you."

"I doubt it. She and David took off to her cabin."

Whoa! That quickly? One dance and she was inviting the guy to her cabin?

So it wasn't that two guys were fighting over me because I was such a spectacular babe. It was because I was the only babe.

I was a little bummed that she hadn't even said good-bye. Truthfully I resented it a little because we'd agreed to come here together, and then she'd taken off with the first eligible guy to come around. My excitement over the evening deflated like a pinpricked balloon.

Michael and I walked back to the table where Cameron had ordered another round of drinks. My daiquiri definitely wasn't a virgin. Although I had a feeling that I was going to remain one for a while longer.

Not that there was anything really wrong with Cameron or Michael. They were fun guys, but I just couldn't see myself getting up close and personal with either one of them.

Besides, I rationalized, I didn't want to hurt either of their feelings by choosing one over the other.

I didn't quite know how to gracefully leave. I was also a little more miffed at Brooke for taking off without even telling me.

"Did Brooke say anything about me before she left?" I asked.

"She told us to take good care of you," Michael said. He wiggled his eyebrows.

"I see. Well, you've certainly done that."

I took a big sip of my daiquiri, and closed my eyes against another brain freeze. I'd gone from fascinating flirt to dead-girl flirt in a heartbeat.

I opened my eyes, and saw Ryan standing between Michael and Cameron. He jerked his head to the side, turned, and headed for the dance floor.

Was that an invitation?

"I'll be right back," I promised, without thinking.

When I caught up with Ryan, I discovered that indeed he'd asked me to dance because he started in close, his gaze holding mine.

"Where's the girl you were with?" I asked. Immediately I wanted to bite off my tongue. It was not cool to admit that I'd noticed him dancing with someone else.

"I'm playing the field," he said with a grin. "So which is it going to be for you? Tweedle Dee or Tweedle Dum?"

I slapped his arm. "They aren't that bad."

"They don't look that good either."

"They're from Oklahoma."

"That explains it then. You know the reason Texas doesn't fall into the Gulf of Mexico is because Oklahoma sucks."

"You only say that because you go to the University of Texas." Oklahoma and Texas were long-standing rivals. Even I knew that. I was fairly certain that Oklahoma had their own Texas jokes.

"Where's Brooke?" he asked.

I felt the heat rush to my face. "She went off with David."

"David?"

"One of the guys we met."

"I see."

I heard the music beginning to wind down, and panic set in.

"Listen, I really don't want to go back to the table and be alone with those guys. Could you walk me out, maybe make it look like we're . . . you know . . . hooking up?"

He grimaced as though he really regretted what he had to say. "If I did that, you might feel like I was looking after you, and I know you don't want that."

I was desperate to get out of there. "I could make an exception this once."

"Well, as a favor to Walter . . ." He slung his arm around my shoulder, and we walked out of the club like we were an item. As soon as we were in the wide corridor, I stepped away from him.

"Thanks."

"Anytime."

"What are you going to do now?"

"Go back in and party some more. I'd invite you to join me, but I know it would cramp your style."

I stared at him a minute, and then I released a deep sigh. "You overheard me talking to Julie last night."

"After I got something to eat, I was going back to join you when I heard you tell her that you didn't want me hanging around."

"So why did you dance with me afterward?"

"Walter expected it."

Ouch! So everything he'd done was because Walter expected it. "Listen, don't take what I said personally. I just had plans for this trip . . ." I shrugged. "I have things that I want to accomplish—"

"Sleeping with a guy."

I closed my eyes. He really knew more than I wanted him to know. I wish I'd never taken a sip of champagne. I opened my eyes. "I want this trip to be memorable, to do things that I've never done before. And yes, making love to a guy is on the list of things that I want to accomplish while I'm on this cruise."

"Parasailing?"

I looked at him. "What?"

"Is parasailing on your list?"

I shook my head. "No."

"Do you only do things that are on your list?"

"I like for things to be planned."

"Maybe you could find a pencil, and add parasailing to your list. I've reserved a boat for tomorrow."

I'd never parasailed, but it sounded like fun. Still . . .

"Why are you asking me?"

"Because I don't want to go by myself."

So it wasn't because he was interested in me, or because he felt like he needed to watch over me to make Walter happy. At the same time it hadn't occurred to me that Ryan would spend time alone if he wasn't looking after me. It should have, but it hadn't. I felt guilty about that, and the fact that he'd overheard me talking to Julie.

"All right. I'll go with you."

"Great. I'll give you the details before we leave the ship in the morning." He jerked his thumb over his shoulder. "I'm going back in to party."

"I'll see you tomorrow then," I said.

He disappeared inside, and I headed up to the Starlight deck.

People were strolling along. I could hear others splashing and shrieking in the pools on another deck.

I was supposed to be having the time of my life. Instead everyone around me was having the time of their life. Brooke was off with David. Ryan was back inside Cruisin' dancing with someone else—or at least I figured he was.

I walked to the railing, and gazed out on the water. It was dark with only the lights from the ship shining over it. The sky was vast and filled with stars.

And I was totally confused.

Ryan was nice, but he didn't act as though he

was interested in me. He'd come to my rescue earlier, and helped me make a graceful exit from the club. But then he'd gone back inside to party, which I was glad he'd done, because I wanted to find someone to have a special night with. I really didn't think it would be a good idea to have a fling with Walter's godson, no matter how nice or good-looking he might be.

We could do the parasailing thing tomorrow. We could keep it casual. Spend a little time together because Walter expected it.

But Ryan knew I had a goal. I was embarrassed that he did know—but he seemed all right with it. And he understood why our hanging around together all the time wouldn't work.

Besides, he probably had a list of things he wanted to do, and I was certain that they didn't include me.

With a sigh I sat on a lounger, and hoped tomorrow would go better than today.

CHAPTER 11

I'd spent my life sleeping in bed alone in a bedroom that I shared with no one. So I couldn't figure out why I felt so lonely as I put on my night boxers and tank, and slipped into bed.

I tried not to think that Ryan might have a girl in his cabin that very minute. And I tried not to think about Brooke hooking up with David. And I tried not to think about that stupid flirtation quiz I had obviously flunked.

It was so different flirting with absolute strangers. They didn't know when you were kidding and when you were serious. They didn't know how to read your body language.

And I certainly didn't know how to read theirs.

Going on this cruise without my best friend in tow sucked big time. I mean, Brooke was fun, but we didn't have a history. She didn't know about the time when Julie and I decided to use hot wax to shape our eyebrows, and ended up with no eyebrows—just swollen, red, hairless areas above our eyes. Or the time we decided to pierce each other's ears with an upholstery needle because our parents wouldn't give us permission to get them pierced. Totally bad idea.

With a sigh I rolled over onto my side.

The phone rang and brought me out of my brooding. I snatched it up. "Hello?"

"Hey, it's Brooke. You weren't at the club when David and I got back."

"Michael said you weren't coming back."

"How would he know? Is he my secretary?"

I shrugged, realized she couldn't see my movements, and said, "I just felt—"

"Abandoned? You probably felt abandoned. I would have. Geez, I'm sorry, Lindsay. Really. David and I just went out to be alone for a while. You know?"

"Yeah, I know," I said, although I really didn't. The nice thing about best friends is that no matter what they say, you always know exactly what they *mean*. With Brooke I didn't really know her well enough to understand what she meant. What she was trying to say or not say.

"So can I come by? I know it's late, but we could talk. You know, have a slumber party," Brooke said.

"I guess so. Sure."

I gave her my cabin number and the location of my cabin before I hung up. I turned on the bedside lamp, clambered out of bed, and slipped on a pair of jersey shorts. I figured my tank was okay as it was.

It was funny how I could be feeling lonely one minute and then excited with apprehension the next.

A knock sounded on my door. Man, that was fast. Her cabin must not be that far away from mine. That could certainly prove beneficial. It would make meeting up with each other a snap. I crossed the cabin, jerked open the door, and froze.

Ryan. Not Brooke.

I fought the urge to cross my arms over my chest. Surely he wouldn't realize I was in PJ's—

"You were already in bed?" he asked.

I leaned against the doorjamb trying to appear unflustered by his question.

"I was, but now I'm not." *I am too clever to live.*

"I was wondering if you wanted to catch a midnight movie."

"Thanks, but Brooke is on her way over." Then I scowled because I'd felt the need to explain myself. My friends, my life, the things I had planned were none of his business.

"She's trouble."

"She's fun. Totally cool. You just haven't given her a chance. You're welcome to join us," I offered.

He laughed. "Thanks, but no thanks."

I was feeling badly. He was alone tonight because I had things on my list that I needed to accomplish without him around. But right now I wasn't flirting with any guys. I wasn't going to make a move on anyone. I was feeling magnanimous. "Why don't you join us? We'll probably just sit out on the deck and talk."

"About toe rings and cramps and how guys just don't get it. I'll pass."

"Well, well, looks like I was interrupting more than sleep," Brooke said as she hurried toward us. "So are you guys an item or not?"

"Not," we both said at the same time.

Ryan grinned. "Tomorrow."

And with that he disappeared into his cabin.

"That guy is so hot. How can you not be an item?" Brooke asked. "And you're right next door to each other? How convenient is that?"

"It's actually turning out to be a little *in*convenient. Come on in."

She gasped as she walked into the cabin. "Wow! You have a terrace! My cabin is like a bed and a bathroom. No view whatsoever. This is totally cool."

She made herself at home, raided the minibar, fixed us both a drink, and headed for the balcony.

We sat out there, with the ocean breeze blowing around us, the lights from the ship glistening off the dark water. It was the perfect place to sit with a guy. The romantic possibilities were endless.

"So explain Ryan."

I glanced over at Brooke. "What?"

She shifted in her chair, brought her feet up beneath her, and started ticking off on her fingers. "He approaches you at the pool. I see you talking to him in the gym."

"You saw that?"

"Yeah. I did. Then he shows up at the club and hardly takes his eyes off you."

"No way!"

"Yes way!"

"He was dancing with someone else."

"And watching you the whole time."

Had he been watching me?

"He's Walter's godson. Walter invited Ryan on the cruise because he thought Ryan would enjoy it, and he thought I needed a buddy. And then I find out that Walter thought I needed a baby-sitter as well. But I can make my own friends and take care of myself." I held my hands out to her. "You're a perfect example."

She sipped her drink. "I still think there's more to it. You've slept with him, right?"

A little voice told me to confess the truth, but the part of me that wanted to be cool simply said, "Yeah, we slept together. But it didn't work out."

"Like me and David."

Probably not, I thought. She and David probably didn't actually sleep.

She took a sip before saying, "David was okay, but he kisses like a lizard."

"A lizard?"

"Yeah, you know, he just stuck his tongue in and out of my mouth. Kinda makes me gag when that's a guy's only move." She shifted in the chair. "So what's the worst kind of kiss you've ever gotten?"

I gave it some serious thought. Then I remembered. "I went on a date with this guy who groaned the entire time we kissed." I laughed. "At first I thought I was hurting him."

"A drama king," she said. "I dated a guy like that once. While he was moaning, he'd bend me over backward—like in the old movies."

"Sounds romantic," I offered.

"Not when he dropped me."

A tiny laugh escaped before I could stop it. "I'm sorry. I know it wasn't funny."

"What about vacuum kissers?" she asked. "You know those guys who suck so hard you have hickeys all over your neck? I dated one guy who was so bad that I had to wear turtlenecks in summer."

"You've dated a lot of guys," I said, unable to hide my astonishment.

"Nothing serious with any of them. Except for my last boyfriend."

"What kind of kisser was he?" I asked.

"Incredible."

"So why didn't it work out?" I asked.

"He liked to spread his kisses around. Kinda like a bee in the spring. You know, can't stick with one flower, just has to spread the pollen around."

"So he was a pollen kisser?"

She laughed. "That's a much nicer name than what I called the jerk. But, yeah, he liked to do a lot of pollinating. I hate that I miss him."

"Concentrate on what a jerk he was," I suggested. I'd never had a serious crush, and I wasn't exactly sure how a girl went about getting over one when things didn't work out. That might explain why I wanted to remain casual with a guy who I wanted to get physical with. No emotional attachment, less hurt.

"I'd probably do better not to think about him at all. David reminded me too much of him."

"I thought David was a lizard kisser."

"He was, but he looked a lot like Chris."

So that was the pollen kisser's name.

"That's probably why I changed my mind about taking him back to my cabin," she said. She glanced over at me. "I mean, I invited him and all, but then I changed my mind, you know. I hate teasing guys, and not following through on the tease."

"Did you explain that you'd just broken up—"

"No way! I told him I was getting seasick."

She sank down in the chair, and lifted her feet to the railing. I did the same.

"I really miss my friends," I said quietly as I gazed out at the vast blackness before us.

"Yeah, me too."

"This cruise is supposed to be my best vacation ever," I said. "But it just hasn't started out that way."

"What would make it the best?" she asked.

"I don't know exactly. It's kinda like I'll know it when I experience it."

We sat in silence for several minutes, each lost in our own thoughts.

"You know the very real possibility exists that we could end up on a desert island out here," Brooke suddenly said.

I didn't think so. As a matter of fact I figured she was being a little melodramatic, but I thought she was probably going somewhere with her comment.

"Who would you want to be with you: Heath Ledger or Ben Affleck?" she asked.

"Heath Ledger."

"I think I'd go with Ben." She sighed. "Or the guy next door."

I sat upright. "Ryan?"

"Yeah. As I may have mentioned, he's really hot."

She stood and leaned against the railing of the balcony. "So should we hit the shops as soon as we dock tomorrow?"

"Sure. But I'm going parasailing in the afternoon."

"Cool! I've always wanted to parasail. I'll invite the guys we met tonight to go with us."

I wasn't really sure how Ryan was going to feel about all the invitations being issued. But how could I possibly tell Brooke, my new best friend, that she wasn't welcome?

"I don't know about inviting the guys we met tonight," I finally managed.

"Come on. It'll be fun."

"Well, the thing is, I'm going with Ryan."

"That makes it even better."

Somehow I didn't think so.

CHAPTER 12

We docked at Charlotte Amalie in the Virgin Islands. From the deck outside my cabin, the capital of St. Thomas looked like a peaceful village with its red-roofed buildings sweeping out into the deep green hills. Ships of all sizes— sloops, yachts, sailboats—rocked gently in the waters within the harbor.

Once Brooke and I left the ship I realized that the calm appearance of the town was deceiving. It was bustling with activity.

"Hey! Jimmy Buffet," Brooke announced as we pass by a shop where the music poured out into the street.

She started walking with little bouncing steps, like she was dancing to the rhythm. I found myself joining her, stepping to the beat, snapping my fingers.

"Is this not totally great?" she asked.

"Totally."

We were headed for the shopping district. Most of the shops were converted warehouses where pirates had reportedly hoarded their stolen goods hundreds of years ago. Everything was quaint, and unlike anything I'd ever seen before.

Our first stop was the Tropicana Perfume Shoppe. The pink-and-white eighteenth-century building was located in the heart of the shopping district. The fragrances were to die for, and sported the names of so many prestigious companies—brand-name labels that I seldom shopped for at home because they were a little out of my price range.

"How about this one?" Brooke asked, holding her wrist up to my nose.

It was a sweet flowery scent. It seemed to go with the Tropics, but I wasn't certain that it went with Brooke. Still, she knew herself better than I did, but I simply didn't see her as sweet.

"I like it," I assured her.

She wrinkled her nose. "I don't know."

She was suddenly a mess of indecision. I didn't blame her; so was I. Far too many scents to choose from. I had a feeling most of the morning was going to be a string of hard decisions.

Brooke dabbed another fragrance on her elbow and sniffed. "I like this one. Do you think Cameron would like it?"

I stared at her. "Cameron?"

She bobbed her head. "Yeah."

"But you and David—"

"Oh, he's history," she said with a flutter of her hand.

"Well, I know, but I think Cameron is his friend, and it just seems like it would be a little awkward."

She shook her head and raised her hand. "The rules are completely different on a cruise. Everyone is a player, and everyone is okay with that."

I didn't think I could be totally okay with that. While I was okay kissing different guys, I only wanted to get intimate with one. Part of the reason why I wasn't willing to seriously consider Ryan as one of those guys because I didn't believe long-term relationships could take root on a cruise, and our paths would pass from time to time once the trip was over. And I would be uncomfortable.

As Brooke had said, things were completely different on a cruise. Sometimes I wasn't even sure who I was.

"Did you invite David to go parasailing with us?" I asked.

"Sure. But he'll be totally cool. He had his chance and blew it. So I'm moving on. He'll move on." She gave me a hard look. "You have to move on, Lindsay. Can't wallow around feeling sorry for yourself just because a guy isn't interested."

"Was David not interested?" I asked.

"Who knows? I didn't give him a chance to say one way or the other. He just wasn't right for me."

She sniffed the latest perfume spritz and sighed. "Chris would like this one."

Chris, her ex. The guy she'd broken up with but still missed.

"Is there a chance you'll get back together with him?"

She scoffed. "No way, Lindsay."

Then why was she worried about whether or not he'd like the perfume? She was trying to forget him with a bunch of different guys, but she'd mentioned him a couple of times already. What was up with that?

"I'm getting this one," she suddenly announced. "How about you?"

I went back to sampling. I wanted something soft, alluring, intriguing. Something I would wear on my special night when I finally met my special man.

Brooke and I were a hodgepodge of scents when we left, each carrying our first purchase. Givenchy adorned her bag; Yves Saint Laurent decorated mine.

Our next stop was a jewelry store. St. Thomas is known for its inexpensive diamonds and emeralds. In fact it's known for its inexpensive everything.

"Get a load of this one!" Brooke squealed, pointing to a necklace. It was fabulous—diamonds and emeralds that just sorta swooped down the neck.

"Where would you wear it?" I asked.

"Who cares? It's a must-have. Absolutely."

I wanted something a bit more practical. I bought an emerald teardrop necklace and matching dangling earrings. Then I spotted the toe rings.

I couldn't resist. I remembered Ryan mentioning that girls talked about toe rings. As if he would know what girls talked about. Just for grins, I bought him one. It probably wouldn't fit him, but that wasn't the point. I just wanted him to know that I was thinking about him.

Whoa! Where did that thought come from?

"What's wrong?" Brooke asked. "You look seriously upset."

"I was just thinking about my friends back home, trying to decide what to get them."

A little white lie that I didn't think would really hurt anyone. If Brooke and I had a history, I could tell her the truth. Julie would understand my confusion, would help me sort out my feelings and frustrations. But Brooke, well, she was just a pal. Someone I'd recently met. Secrets and yearnings weren't something I was ready to share with her.

"You should probably get them something local," Brooke suggested.

I'd almost forgotten what she was talking about. "Good idea."

I ended up with dangling bracelets for my friends—and the toe ring for Ryan.

Brooke and I scoured through the shops with our wallets getting thinner and the bags we carried getting heavier. Candles, more jewelry, clothes. While shopping on the islands I planned to only use the money I'd earned and saved for this trip, but there were too many wonderful things to choose from.

Although we would have liked to have shopped until we dropped, we didn't have time. We'd even shopped for tattoos, but I hadn't purchased anything there, nor had I done any piercing.

I had decided that having any needles placed into my skin could wait until I got home and could be sure the establishment was hygienic and up on the health laws. No reason to get carried away so early into vacation.

We barely had time to return to the ship, cart our bags to our cabins, change into shorts and a bathing-suit top, and head back into town. We hooked up with the guys at Enrique's Parasailing.

I'd neglected to mention to Ryan that others would be joining us when he'd given me the reservation information that morning. Now he looked exactly as I figured he would when he discovered the truth: not happy.

And I didn't blame him. I should have told him what had developed, and given him the option of telling me to forget the whole thing before we had an audience.

"We're taking dumb, dumber, and dumbest along?" he asked.

"I invited Brooke, Brooke invited them. The guys aren't really that bad. I was thinking the more the merrier." I furrowed my brow. "Although I'm surprised they were able to get seats on the same boat as us. I figured there would have to be some adjustments made."

"Not when I reserved the boat."

I lifted my eyebrows. "You reserved the whole boat? Not just a couple of spaces?"

He shrugged. "Walter took care of it."

"He is way too generous."

"Tell me about it. He likes to go first class, and he can afford it, so why not?"

"I guess. I just always feel badly spending his money. Will it be a problem for these guys to come along?"

"I guess not."

He didn't sound utterly convinced or convincing.

"Hey, look!" Cameron called out. "We got food here. Dog, this is going to be too cool."

I looked at Ryan. "You brought food?"

"I thought you might be hungry after shopping all morning," Ryan said.

"Oh." I felt uncomfortable with his consideration, and wondered if he'd been planning for us to picnic somewhere. I really should have checked with him about inviting people before I let Brooke take over the excursion.

I wanted to make things up to Ryan. I reached into my pocket. "I bought you a present."

"You did?"

He brightened up so much with my pronouncement that I felt guiltier because the present was supposed to be a joke. Still, I pressed it into his palm.

"A ring?" he said in disbelief.

"A toe ring."

He chuckled, crouched, and slipped it onto his second toe. He was wearing baggy shorts and sandals. Somehow the ring seemed to belong.

"Hey, not bad," he said with a grin.

"It was supposed to be a joke," I admitted, "because you said girls talk about toe rings. But it really does look good on you."

"Does this mean we're going steady?" he asked.

My eyes grew big and round. "No way. That idea never crossed my mind."

"Are you guys going to mess around all day or what?" Brooke asked. "I'm ready to fly the friendly skies."

We all climbed aboard the speed boat. We met Pete, who would be driving the boat, and Rick, who would be helping us harness up. We took our seats and headed out toward the blue waters.

"Anyone parasailed before?" I asked.

"No way, dude," David said.

The others all shook their heads. Everyone except Ryan.

He was sitting beside me, and I couldn't help thinking that if he wasn't Walter's godson, I'd've shown a lot more interest in him. But in all fairness I couldn't do that when I wanted something short-term for the cruise. And he certainly hadn't given any indication that he wanted anything more than someone to pal around with. I figured our getting involved would only lead to our being uncomfortable around each other when our paths crossed at school or at Walter's.

"You've parasailed," I said to him, finding myself intrigued by him when I knew I shouldn't be.

"Catalina and Mackinac Islands, in the Pacific and on the Great Lakes. And of course, off the coast of Texas."

"You must like it then," I said.

"It's totally cool."

I really thought Ryan was being a good sport with the unexpected company. Everyone was dipping into the ice chest, helping themselves to drinks as we cruised out beyond the harbor.

The boat slowed. Rick crouched down in the middle of where we were all sitting. His flowered shirt was completely unbuttoned, his baseball cap on backward. He was barefoot and deeply tanned. I figured most of these guys were envying him his job. Casual, in the sun, and on the water. What could be better?

"Okay," Rick began, "you paid to have the boat for two hours. Takes about thirty minutes to get you up and to get you back down, so some of you are going to have to go in tandem."

"I'll go with Lindsay," Ryan said before anyone else could get a word out.

I knew he'd responded quickly simply because he was watching out for me, as Walter had requested. I might have objected if I'd been interested in any of the other guys traveling with us.

"How exactly does 'in tandem' work?" I asked.

"You're harnessed together and go up at the same time," Rick explained.

Harnessed together? I darted a quick glance over at Ryan. I had a vision of us plummeting into the sea like a sack of rocks. I looked back at Rick. "Won't we weigh too much?"

"Nah. You'll be fine." He gave me a wink. "Now which of you guys is going to pair up with the other babe?"

The "other" babe? That meant he considered me a babe. I gave him a closer inspection, but couldn't quite see me hanging around with a beach bum. Not that he was a total bum.

He was working. I couldn't figure out if he was a student just here for the summer, or someone who'd come for vacation and decided not to leave. He probably spent a lot of time doing his own parasailing, or snorkeling, or wind surfing. Out on the ocean almost every water sport I could imagine was going on. For someone who was into outdoor water activities, life here would be quite idyllic. Playing all the time.

After much discussion, shoving around like two-year-olds, the guys Brooke had invited finally decided that Michael would be the one to go up with her.

David shoved Ryan's shoulder. "So how come we didn't have any discussion on who gets to go up with Lindsay?"

"I called it."

"Yeah, dog, but that's not fair. None of us had a chance."

Ryan leaned toward him. "Tell you what, *dog*. You pay for the boat rental, and you can take her up."

David gave him a cocky grin. "How much, man?"

Ryan leaned closer and, with a low voice that I couldn't hear, revealed the amount.

"Dude!" David said. "No chick is worth that." He furrowed his brow. "Do we, like, need to chip in something?"

Ryan shook his head. "Don't sweat it. I've got it covered."

Which left me to wonder who really was paying for the boat rental: Ryan or Walter? Not that it really mattered. Ryan had made the arrangements, and was being a good sport about extra people cutting into his time. And it really wasn't anyone's business if Walter, as Ryan had suggested earlier, was picking up the tab.

"All righty," Rick said with a clap of his hands. "Let's do the singles first. Dudes, put on your life jackets."

Cameron went first. It was interesting to watch them harness him in. I couldn't image how it was going to work with me and Ryan going together.

I also didn't like to admit that I thought it might be fun to go up with someone. Especially Ryan.

"So what are you doing tonight?" I asked, trying to be a little friendlier.

"Checking out the clubs. You?"

I shrugged. "Probably the same."

"Definitely the same," Brooke said leaning toward both of us. "We don't leave port until late tonight. We might as well party with the natives for a while. Ryan, you want to come with us?"

"These clowns coming?" Ryan asked.

"Hey, dude," David said. "We're not clowns."

"Sure, they'll come," Brooke said, totally ignoring David's comment.

Which I thought was wise. The last thing we needed was someone to go overboard, and I figured in a scuffle between David and Ryan David would be the one who went into the water.

"The more the merrier," Brooke continued. "Maybe we'll even meet some more people to add to the crowd."

"I'll think about it," Ryan said.

"You do that," Brooke said. "Just give me a nudge if you want to join us."

The boat started moving faster, picking up speed. Rick started reeling Cameron out.

"Wahoo!" Cameron yelled.

I watched him going up and out, higher and higher.

"Oh, wow," I said. "What happens if he falls in the water?"

"We go back for him," Rick said.

I had a horrible thought rush through my mind. "Are there sharks out there?"

"None that'll bite," Rick said, grinning.

The rumble of the boat, the whipping of the wind, and the raucous laughter of the gang that Brooke had brought along made it difficult to really talk as we cruised along. As I watched each person go up, sail, and then come back down, guilt nagged at me. Ryan had made the arrangements for this outing, and we'd all barged in like bulls in a china shop.

I watched Brooke and Michael go up. It looked like the ultimate in fun. Brooke stood in front of Michael, and he placed his arms around her. The line was reeled out, and they traveled higher. Michael leaned around, and kissed Brooke on the cheek. Cameron and David grunted like a couple of seals.

"Lucky dude!" one of them shouted.

I glanced over at Ryan who seemed to be taking it all in stride. Still, I felt guilty, and decided to try to talk with him.

I leaned close. "Look, if you want to go alone, I completely understand. It's not like I have to go."

He tipped his head to the side so we were even closer. "Don't worry. I won't try to kiss you while we're up there."

My mouth dropped open. That idea had *so* not occurred to me.

All right. Maybe it had . . . a little. I mean, it would be incredible to be doing all this with someone I really cared about.

"I just thought you might want to go alone. That was your original plan, right?" I asked.

He shrugged.

What did that mean?

"You're here," he said. "No sense in not going up."

His lack of enthusiasm made me feel like an

anchor around his neck, dragging him down into the deep blue waters.

Rick started reeling Brooke and Michael back in. Oh my gosh. Had a half an hour passed by already?

I started taking deep breaths. The last thing I wanted to do was hyperventilate.

"Getting nervous?" Ryan asked me.

I forced myself to smile. "No. I've just never done this before."

He grinned at me. "You'll love it."

Brooke was beaming broadly as her feet touched down on the deck. Her face was flushed with excitement, and I figured mine was about to do the same.

"Totally awesome!" she screamed.

As soon as the harnesses were removed, Michael grabbed Brooke and kissed her. She threw her head back, and laughed like some starlet in a movie. Dramatic and fun-loving.

I wondered if Ryan would change his mind and decide to kiss me when our trip up was over. No way was he going to do that. I was Walter's new daughter, who he was supposed to watch over—not a girl he was supposed to get serious about.

The boat slowed and then idled while Rick helped Ryan and me get into the harness. My back was against Ryan's chest. He put his arms around me. I put my arms over his. It was silly, but it made me feel as though I was anchored to something. Gave me a sense of security. And I needed that because my heart was pounding like a sledgehammer.

I heard clicks and snaps as Rick hooked me and Ryan up. I felt a tug here, a tug there. And then Rick was backing away.

"Okay, just relax," Rick said.

I took a deep breath and nodded. "I'm relaxed."

"All righty, then, here we go."

The boat revved up, the wind caught the parachute, and I felt myself being lifted— pulled—up into the sky and away from the deck of the boat.

"Relax, Lindsay," Ryan said near my ear. "We're perfectly safe."

"Perfectly?"

"Yeah. The worst that will happen is that we'll get caught in a crosswind, and the chute will collapse."

"And then?"

"We just go into the water. You swim, right?"

I glanced over my shoulder at him as much as possible. "Of course."

We floated upward, the tether, which kept us secured to the craft, was being released bit by bit as the boat gained speed. I felt carefree, weightless, high.

"Cool!" I called out.

I had a bird's-eye view of the island and the ocean. It was incredible.

"Look down," Ryan ordered.

I obeyed, and my stomach did a little somersault. I hadn't realized how high we'd ascended in such a short time. I was even more amazed by all that was below me. The Caribbean waters were so clear that I could see the outline of coral reefs.

Gorgeous. It was so gorgeous. I was totally in awe.

I looked back at Ryan. "Oh my gosh! It's amazing!"

"It's completely different looking down on it from here," he said.

"No kidding." I couldn't wait until we got to the Cayman Islands, where I planned to do some snorkeling. "Thank you for inviting me."

Then he did the most remarkable, unexpected thing. He cupped the side of my head, kept my face turned toward him, leaned forward, and kissed me.

CHAPTER 13

Ryan *kissed me.*

Dangling high above the water had been a total rush, but add to that his hot, slow kiss . . . I'd felt as though I could actually touch the clouds.

I hadn't wanted the kiss or the parasailing to end. But both had to eventually. Sitting in the boat across from him, I wondered why he'd kissed me. Had he simply gotten caught up in the wonder of being near the clouds—or was there more to it?

Was he interested in me? Or was I still only someone he was supposed to look after? Surely he didn't think Walter expected him to kiss me.

So why had he?

He certainly hadn't given any impression that it was a big deal. As a matter of fact he was acting a little as though he was embarrassed by what he'd done. He simply sat there in silence as the boat headed back into shore. How interesting.

And wild Lindsay was too shy to ask him why he kissed her. Maybe because a part of me feared he'd done it out of some sort of misguided obligation or some sort of male one-upmanship. Michael had kissed Brooke, so Ryan had felt a need to kiss me.

I should ask him. I really should. Yeah, right. Like that was going to happen.

The boat pulled up to the dock. Everyone scrambled out, except for Ryan, who was talking with Rick. I thought maybe he was discussing the payment arrangements.

"Thanks, Ryan," I called out.

He nodded and waved. "I'll catch up with you later."

I wondered if he really would. Brooke hooked her arm through mine, and started marching us away from the dock.

"Come on. We need to get back to the ship so we can get ready to hit the bars," she said.

"What about Ryan?" I asked.

"He said he'd catch up."

But once we'd moved beyond the dock and down the shoreline a ways, she pulled me aside, moved her sunglasses down the bridge of her nose, and glared at me over the top of them. "What aren't you telling me about you and Ryan?"

I stared at her. "I don't know what you're talking about."

"That kiss. What was up with that kiss?"

"You saw it, huh?"

"It was a little hard to miss. And it went on forever."

I'd felt that way at the time—that it was going on forever—but I'd also thought that maybe my senses were skewed because we were up high where the oxygen was thin.

"I didn't think you were interested in him," Brooke said, impatiently as though she'd given up on my answering her question.

"I'm not." *Much.*

If only he weren't Walter's godson. . . .

"Well, you sure could have fooled me," Brooke said.

I was beginning to think that maybe I was fooling myself as well.

"I can't believe Mr. Stick-In-the-Mud kissed you," Brooke said.

Brooke and I were strolling through the gaily lit streets of St. Thomas. We'd returned to the ship, and changed into tank tops, loosely flowing skirts, and sandals for our night on the town.

And she was still talking about Ryan's kiss. Not that I could blame her. I was still thinking about it myself.

"Ryan isn't a stick-in-the-mud," I retorted.

"Well, he wasn't exactly Mr. Party Guy on the boat this afternoon," Brooke asked.

"We crashed his party," I reminded her. "He invited me, I invited you, and you invited the guys we met last night. So maybe he was a little bummed. Maybe he had a right to be."

She shrugged. "Whatever."

I was a little ticked off at her for not appreciating everything Ryan had given us this afternoon. There was a part of me that liked Brooke, and a part of me that thought Brooke was all about Brooke. That maybe she thought the world revolved around her.

Not that we don't all have moments like that, but Brooke seemed to think everything centered on her all the time.

She hooked her arm through mine. "The afternoon is over, and it's time to find some guys to warm us through the night."

Warm us through the night. Yes, I was so down with that. And just like that I decided to overlook some of Brooke's more irritating aspects, and to just appreciate the party girl in her. And hope that some of the party girl would rub off on me, because I thought only a major distraction was going to cause me to stop thinking about Ryan's kiss.

Music filtered out into the night as Brooke and I checked out the nightlife. She was totally into it, snapping her fingers, singing a few lines of a tune whenever we heard a song that we knew.

I was completely loose and relaxed when Brooke grabbed my hand and led me into a thatched-roofed building. From the look at the people inside, no one dressed up for island night life apparently.

"This way," Brooke called back to me as she marched forward, unafraid.

We wended our way among the crowds until we reached the veranda and courtyard. The islands were known for their steel-pan bands, and here the music from a live band resonated around us.

"Over here," Brooke said, pointing to a small table.

We'd barely sat down when a waitress came over to take our orders. Brooke ordered two beers before I could say anything.

Brooke was bobbing her shoulders up and down, rolling them around, in rhythm with the music.

"Is this not cool?" she asked.

"Absolutely."

The waitress returned with our drinks. Brooke picked a bottle up, then turned back to give her attention to the band. I smiled at the waitress, dug into my pocket, and retrieved some money to place on her tray. I was beginning to notice that when it was time to pay for things, Brooke was usually preoccupied—watching something else or conveniently talking with someone.

I didn't mind. I didn't have any expenses on this trip except for what I spent on the islands, and I'd been saving my money for some time.

Once the waitress walked away, Brook turned back to me and tapped the neck of her bottle against mine. "To good times."

Lifting my bottle, I returned the gesture.

This was so unlike anything that my buds and I had done before, that I was feeling a little like a stranger in a strange land. And yet, I loved it. The sounds, the atmosphere, the people who continually wandered in and out.

It was obvious that most of the people were tourists. Too many were sunburned or had zinc oxide covering their noses. Probably from doing much of the same things that we'd done today.

I watched as a couple of guys at one table were chugalugging bottles of beer without stopping, their friends cheering them on. I figured the winner was the one who finished first.

A resounding cheer went up as a dark-haired guy slammed his empty bottle on the table and released a large belch. Everyone was patting him on the back. He wore a lei around his neck. Only one button on his Hawaiian shirt was buttoned. That seemed to be about as dressed up as he got. He caught me looking at him and grinned.

In an effort to improve my flirtation technique, I grinned back.

"So how would you describe Ryan's kiss?" Brooke asked.

I jerked my attention away from the hottie, and stared at Brooke. "What?"

"Ryan. When he kissed you this afternoon, what was it like?"

I took a swig of beer, not really liking the taste. I decided when the waitress stopped by, I'd order a margarita. For now, I needed some time to think up an answer to Brooke's question. I'd never shared my experiences with guys with my best friends, and I felt a little awkward revealing anything to Brooke. On the other hand, once this trip was over, we'd probably never see each other again.

"It was nice," I said.

Her eyes got big and round. "Nice? Nice is when a guy gives you the answers to your math homework. Get a little more specific."

"It was just a kiss. It just wouldn't be fair to try to describe it."

"Toadlike?"

"Definitely not."

"Slobbery?"

"No." I gave up trying to get her to stop asking me about the kiss. "It was perfect, okay?"

"Okay." She grinned. "See, that wasn't so hard, was it? Honestly, Lindsay, you need to learn to open up. I sense that you have a lot of repressed sexuality."

"What are you? A psychiatrist?"

"I'm an observer of human nature." Brooke looked back over the crowds as though she was extremely pleased with something.

"Come on, let's dance!" she shouted.

"We don't have dance partners," I pointed out.

"Who's going to notice in that crowd?"

I followed her out to the patio where people were dancing—not always together, not always as couples. It didn't really seem to matter.

The important thing was to move with the music, sidle up to someone, make eye contact, and move away to the next person. Brooke seemed completely comfortable doing exactly that. I was more or less dancing by myself. No way could I go up and touch my shoulder to a stranger's.

Then I felt a nudge against my shoulder and turned. There was the beer-guzzling winner.

He grinned. "Aren't you traveling on *The Enchantment*?"

I nodded. "Yeah."

"Thought I saw you at the club last night. I'm Chad."

"Lindsay."

We were dancing, moving, even as we were talking.

"So where are you from?" he asked.

I laughed at the now unoriginal but so familiar question." "Dallas."

"New Orleans."

We continued to move in rhythm to the beat of the band. Chad was cute. Dark hair and eyes. Up close, it appeared that he'd decided to give his razor a vacation as well, because he had stubble on his chin that seemed scraggly and out of place.

"So you partying loose?" he asked. "Or are you hooked up with someone?"

"Well, I came with a friend."

I pointed over to where Brooke was dancing between two guys. One I recognized as the beer-guzzling loser. I have to admit that I felt rather pleased that the winner had chosen me. Although I suppose even the word "winner" can be a relative term.

I didn't want to contemplate on the fact that Brooke'd attracted two guys to my one. She was definitely vixen flirtation.

Chad grinned. "Only her? No dude?"

"No dude."

"Cool."

We continued to dance. Chad was nice enough. He had a cute, sexy grin. Orthodontist money, well spent. But I didn't feel that skip-a-heartbeat-catch-my-breath double take that I had when I'd met Ryan.

As the music momentarily paused, Chad took my hand to keep me in the dance area. As the music started up again, and we picked up the rhythm of the beat, I told myself that he was a lot of fun.

Because he *was* cute. There was absolutely nothing wrong with the guy. I kept telling myself that maybe he was the one. However, myself kept replying, "Don't think so."

But I couldn't figure out why not.

Brooke made her way over to me, her two guys in tow.

"This is Marc with a C, and Shooter," Brooke said, introducing her dance partners.

I had to tilt my head back to look into Shooter's eyes. With his hands he made a little motion like someone holding a basketball and then making a free throw.

"Basketball," he explained.

"He claims to have good hands," Brooke said, leaning into him. "I like a guy with good hands."

"I have the best," Shooter said.

"Marc and Shooter are staying on the same ship that we are," Brooke said. It turned out that the guys we'd been dancing with were traveling together.

"So we're going to blow this joint," Brooke said. "Are you coming?"

"Where?"

"Who knows? Wherever the mood strikes."

"Sure."

Chad slung his arm across my shoulders, as though to lay claim on me. I shouldn't have been bothered by his attention, but it just seemed like a little too much intimacy too fast.

But wasn't that what I wanted?

No, what I wanted was to meet someone with whom I immediately bonded and felt amazingly comfortable with. An image of Ryan jumped into my mind, and I shoved it back out. Ryan and I would only feel more awkward if we tried to become intimate. I had a feeling he knew that as much as I did, which was the reason why he'd been so quiet on the boat ride back to the dock. Whatever had possessed him to kiss me to begin with was a mystery, but he'd obviously regretted it.

Chad was nice and fun, but I didn't feel that connection with him that I was looking for.

Still, he was a good dancer. And a heck of a beer guzzler.

The five of us roamed the streets of St. Thomas, hitting one club after another. Sometimes just sitting at a table, drinking margaritas, and listening to music. Sometimes dancing like crazy.

No rhyme or reason. Just whatever mood struck us. Or, rather, struck Brooke.

I was beginning to think she was ADD, because she never sat still for long.

It grew late, and I knew my time in St. Thomas was coming to a close.

People began meandering back toward the ship. Chad still had his arm across my shoulders, though I was beginning to think that he was using me more as a crutch than anything else. He was a little unsteady on his feet after winning every beer-guzzling contest that he and his buds had competed in tonight.

"We've got a little time. Let's walk the shoreline," Brooke suggested, a guy on either side of her.

They wove down the shore, laughing and giggling. It was funny to watch because I didn't think any of them could have walked a straight line if their lives depended on it.

Chad and I reached the water's edge, and he leaned on me a little heavily.

"You're the best, Lindsay," he said, his words a little slurred. "How about a kiss?"

Where was the spontaneity in that? But I was determined to be a good sport. And he did have that killer smile.

I turned my face up toward him, watched as his eyes rolled back, felt his arm slipping off my shoulders . . .

And screeched as he hit the sand in an ungraceful heap.

CHAPTER 14

Our walk along the shoreline left a lot to be desired. Chad's friends—who weren't much steadier on their feet than he'd been—struggled to haul him back to the boat. Brooke thought the whole thing was hilarious.

"Aren't they fun?" she asked, as we followed the guys back to the dock.

"Absolutely. I don't know when I've enjoyed watching a guy pass out more," I said sarcastically.

She nudged my shoulder with hers. "Okay, I'll admit that part wasn't cool. But you gotta expect to see a few guys pass out when you're on the islands. That's what it's all about."

Drinking until you literally dropped? It wasn't exactly how I planned for my island adventures to go. Although I had quite a buzz going right now, I was fairly certain that I was still walking a straight line.

When we arrived back at the ship, I was feeling a tad restless. But I wasn't really in the mood to go clubbing.

"I'm going to sit on deck for a while," I told Brooke.

"I'll join you."

I had figured she'd go off with Shooter, so I was surprised when she decided to come with me to the top deck. Only a few people were still up there, so we settled onto loungers.

Isolated, staring up at the stars.

Brooke sighed. "I wish I could live on an island forever. It's such fun."

"Don't you think it would get old after awhile?" I asked.

"Never."

I wasn't so sure, though. I mean, I loved shopping, listening to the bands, parasailing, dancing, meeting guys. But they were all part of vacation, and what made vacation fun was knowing that I was having experiences that I wouldn't normally have.

If that made any sense.

It was the uniqueness of it all.

"There's something incredibly peaceful about being on the ocean," I said.

"You've got that right."

"Brooke, are you in school?"

"Sophomore. Community college."

"Do you have a major?"

"Partying."

I shifted in the chair. "No, seriously. I know you like to party, but I don't know anything else about you."

Other than she'd broken up with Chris, but I didn't want to get her thoughts going down that path.

"There's not much more to know. I'm all about partying, enjoying life, getting the most out of it."

"I'm so dull next to you."

"Are you kidding me?" she asked. "You're fun, Lindsay. I wouldn't be hanging out with you if you weren't fun."

"That's a ringing endorsement."

"It is. You've got no idea."

I suppose I really didn't have any idea how much fun I was. Maybe I was selling myself short. After all so far on this cruise, I'd danced with several guys, kissed a guy, and slept with a guy (sort of).

"The guys we met tonight . . . which one did you like best?" she asked.

"Chad is the only one I really spent much time with."

"His collapsing sort of ruins his appeal," she said.

"Definitely."

"I don't know why guys can't figure out when they've reached their limits on drinking." She spread out her arms. "I mean. Here we are, two hot chicks, alone because those boys have to put their passed-out buddy to bed. How lame is that? We could still be out."

"The clubs onboard are still open."

"All the good guys are probably taken by now."

We sat for a while, just watching the sky. Eventually the ship sounded its horn, and we began moving into the night.

"So tomorrow is an onboard day and night," Brooke finally said. "Why don't we meet poolside around two?"

After spending all day with Brooke, I was ready for some alone time, and I could easily get that in the morning. "I'm down with that."

"I'll let the guys know."

My eyes widened. "Which guys?"

She grinned. "All of them. I believe in bringing the party with me."

She stood. "I had a great time today, Lindsay.

See you tomorrow."

"'Night, Brooke."

I shifted my body, trying to get more comfortable on the lounger. I was still too restless to go to bed. I suppose I could have sat on the balcony outside my cabin, but I was in the mood for a lot of openness.

I couldn't help but think about the movie *Titanic*. The romance that had taken place aboard that ship had me sitting through the movie three times. Of course watching Leonardo Di Caprio wasn't any hardship either.

I suppose a part of me had thought that I'd easily find a romance similar to the one in the movie, on a cruise ship.

But it wasn't easy meeting people. The guys we'd met tonight could just have easily been traveling on another ship that was touring the Caribbean, and our paths would never again cross.

Tomorrow, however, would be another day. Maybe I'd have a bit more luck at meeting Mr. Perfect-for-One-Night.

Closing my eyes I gave some thought to what I was really looking for in a guy, but before I could develop a clear image, I felt myself drifting into sleep. I didn't have the energy or the desire to rouse myself and return to my cabin. Just a few minutes. Just a few minutes of rest. That was all I really wanted.

I woke up to find a large beach towel draped over me, and the sun easing over the horizon. It was really gorgeous, painting the sky with deep pastels. I knew by their very nature that pastels weren't bright colors but when nature was doing the artistry, there was a brilliance to the hue that was indescribable.

Oh, gosh, it was simply wonderful. I sat up straighter, stretched, and stilled.

Ryan was sitting in the chair beside me.

"What are you doing here?" I blurted.

"I wanted to get in a morning jog before it got crowded. Spotted you. Did you lose your key again?"

I wrinkled my nose at him. "I didn't lose my key before."

"Okay, then, did you give your key to someone else, and forget to reclaim it?"

I covered my mouth as I released a wide yawn. "No. I was just sitting here last night, enjoying the peace and quiet." I shrugged. "Guess I fell asleep."

I sat up a little more, and grimaced as my previously still and cramped muscles revolted. A lounge chair was not a good place to spend the night.

"Stiff?" Ryan asked.

"And more: cramped, sore, and achy," I admitted. "I'm going to have to go get a muscle melt."

"A muscle melt?"

"A massage the spa gives. It melts the muscles."

"Turn around. I'll work on your shoulders."

I couldn't figure out why I felt uncomfortable with his offer. It was innocent enough, and I really was feeling like my body absolutely didn't want to move this morning.

"You don't have to do that," I said. "They have professionals onboard."

He sat up and dropped his legs over the edge of the lounger. "Yeah, but they're not up this early, and I've got nothing else to do right now. Come on."

Tucking my feet up beneath me, I turned on the lounger so my back was to him. Since I was wearing a tank top, most of my shoulders were exposed, and I could feel the heat of his hands against my skin as he began to work the stiffness out of my neck and shoulders. It was nice. He was nice.

Suddenly his hands stilled on my shoulders. "So, how many things are left on your list?" he asked.

"Several."

His hands started working their magic again. "What got checked off last night?" he asked.

"Drinking margaritas. What did you do?"

"Hit the clubs."

"I didn't see you." I tilted my head to the side. Felt the muscles loosening up. This was a great thing to wake up to.

"Meet anyone interesting?" he asked.

"We met a couple of guys. Three really. How about you?"

"Yeah, I spent some time with a girl."

That comment bothered me a lot more than I wanted it to. So yesterday's kiss had really meant nothing to him. On the other hand I'd kissed him back, and I'd spent time with other guys last night. It was better if it meant nothing. Absolutely. Or at least that's what I told myself.

"Have you seen Mom or Walter lately?"

"Nope, and I haven't been looking for them."

He patted my shoulders as though he was finished. "Don't forget we have tickets for a show tonight."

I clambered off the lounger and stretched. Passengers were starting to come on deck. I could see people walking and jogging on the track.

"What time?" I asked.

"I'll knock on your door at eight. We can just walk to it together."

"What about Brooke? Did you get her ticket?"

"Yeah, but I didn't get tickets for her traveling entourage."

"I'll let her know. And thanks for the massage."

"You're welcome." He picked up the beach towel that had been draped over me, and walked away.

I watched him disappear. My mind obviously hadn't begun to function yet because it took me a minute to remember that he'd spotted me when he was jogging. Had covered me with his beach towel.

How many people carried a beach towel when they went jogging? He was taking this looking-after-me-at-Walter's-request a little too seriously. And I found myself wondering why that notion didn't bother me as much as it once had.

CHAPTER 15

The Enchantment **Day Four**

Brooke had said that she liked to bring the party with her, and she absolutely did. I was sitting on the deck of the ship near the off-limits-to-kids-pool when she arrived with her entourage, as Ryan referred to them.

Six guys following after her like puppies hoping for a dog-biscuit treat. It was kinda amusing to watch.

She spotted me and waved enthusiastically. Then she was heading toward me. I'd arrived before it had begun to get crowded, and had been able to claim a couple of loungers, but no way did I know that I needed to claim eight. It seemed inconsiderate for our group to take up so many, especially when I hadn't been certain that Brooke would bring everyone.

I suppose I shouldn't have doubted her, but now I wondered where everyone was going to sit.

Apparently the guys were okay with the ground or the edge of a lounger because as soon as Brooke claimed hers, they were sitting around both of us. There didn't seem to be any rhyme or reason to where they sat.

In high school I'd done a lot of group dating. You know, where several guys and girls go out together. Sometimes you pair up, sometimes you don't. It took a lot of the pressure off to hook up with one person, and prevented that one-on-one awkwardness that sometimes happened before you were really sure if one-on-one would even work for you.

But we'd always had as many guys as we had girls so no one would feel like they were the odd-one out. With Brooke I sometimes felt as though she'd hooked up with me so she'd have someone to foist the unwanteds off on.

Okay, I'm sure she didn't mean for the results to appear that way. Brooke didn't give each guy an equal amount of attention, and whoever wasn't the flavor of the moment tended to drift over toward me.

I just didn't have Brooke's knack for blowing a guy off while still leading him on. But I suppose that was all part of being a vixen flirt, and she had the style down pat.

The guys didn't seem to mind—if they even

noticed what was going on. Sometimes guys are totally clueless.

"You know, I'm really craving a smoothie," Brooke said.

"I'll get it!" Michael and Shooter said at the same time, both jumping to their feet.

"You want something, Lindsay?" Chad asked.

"Yeah." I reached for my fanny pack.

"Don't worry about it. I'll get it," he said. "What do you want?"

I ordered a strawberry-banana smoothie. All the guys traipsed off as though they couldn't handle getting the drinks alone. Or maybe they didn't trust leaving anyone behind, and had an unwritten code that no one could stay with us if even one of them had to leave.

"Aren't they great?" Brooke asked.

"But which one do you like?"

"Oh, I like them all. You're welcome to share."

"Share?" I asked, a little dumbfounded.

"Sure. We're on vacation. It's not like we're going to get serious about any of them."

I'd never shared guys before, and I wasn't certain that I wanted to now. I mean, I didn't mind us all hanging around together, but I didn't want a guy thinking he could hook up with Brooke and then come over and be with me. Or that after being with me, he was free to move on to Brooke.

It gave me an icky feeling to even think about it.

"You know, Brooke, I'm not really into sharing."

She rolled her eyes. "That's so boring, Lindsay."

"I don't think so."

She did a little impatient shoulder-roll. "All right. So who do you want? Once I know, I'll stay away from him."

Gosh, that put me on the spot.

"I'm not really sure," I admitted.

"All right then, we'll play the field until you are. And meet other guys along the way."

"More guys?"

"Sure, why not?"

I guess there was really no reason not to meet more guys. And maybe I would meet one who instantly sent my heart racing. Speaking of guys who sent my heart racing . . .

"Oh, listen, we have tickets to the cabaret

show tonight. You can meet us outside the theater at eight."

Brooke arched a brow. "And who exactly is *us*?"

"Me and Ryan."

"You know, for someone you're not interested in, you sure hang around with him a lot."

"It's like I told you: He's my new stepfather's godson. I can't ignore him completely."

"Are you sure that's all there is to it?"

No, I wasn't sure. Ryan was nice, and I liked him, but he seriously interfered with my plans for this cruise. I'd even begun to consider changing them. Spending more time with Ryan, because here I was, fourth day into the trip, and I hadn't met any guy who I was even contemplating as a possible fling prospect.

I was going to give myself one more day, and if I didn't meet someone who intrigued me just a little . . . I wasn't sure exactly what I was going to do. I was determined to complete all the items on my list. But I wanted the last to be special.

The guys returned in force, with smoothies for everyone. We sipped our drinks, and ate the nachos that a couple of the guys had brought over. We got into a heated discussion on whether or not we should scuba dive or snorkel when we got to the Grand Cayman.

It seemed the guys that Brooke had latched on to had plans to hang around for the long haul. They were nice enough, so I wasn't bothered by it, but since none had really set my heart to pounding, I was a little worried that they might limit my abilities to find the right guy.

"Who's up for some rock climbing?" Michael asked.

I had to admit that I'd been eyeing the climbing wall. I'd seen them at various sporting-goods stores, but had never ventured onto one.

"I am," I told him.

"But it'll be hot and sweaty," Brooke whined.

"It'll be fun," I assured her.

Besides, we were on vacation in the Caribbean. Hot and sweaty was part of the vacation. Even with tropical breezes, the weather was warm.

Brooke let the guys taunt and tease her. I was beginning to think that her lack of enthusiasm was more for show than anything. A way to get attention.

Eventually they convinced her to give it a try. We gathered up our pool stuff, and headed to the wall. There wasn't much of a line, which surprised me.

Only one guy was climbing, and I'd recognize him anywhere.

Ryan.

He was near the top, probably close to twenty feet above the ground, testing hand- and footholds before he went any higher. I'd watched enough rock climbing at various stores that I knew it was a lot harder than it looked.

"Wow," Brooke said in a respectful, hushed tone. "He is, like, totally in shape."

He was wearing shorts and a tank top similar to the one he'd worn in the gym. The muscles in his legs and arms looked almost as hard as the wall he was scaling.

"Why is he just hanging there?" Brooke asked.

"He's trying to find the right hold so he can move up," Shooter said. "The higher you go, the harder it gets. Man, I've only been able to get about two-thirds of the way up a wall before totally losing it."

"And what happens then?" Brooke asked. "I mean, when you lose it?"

"You're on a pulley," Shooter said, "so you

dangle in the air for a while, and then they bring you down."

I heard their conversation, but my eyes were glued on Ryan. He finally made his move, reaching and stretching up. I was totally impressed. He wasn't rushing it, wasn't trying to grandstand or impress anyone other than himself. He simply took his moves slowly and steadily.

The guys who were with us started chanting, "Go! Go! Go!" while they slowly clapped.

Ryan glanced down, and it was like his gaze found me. I was afraid to move, to speak, to do anything that might distract him. I knew he was perfectly safe up there, tethered to the pulley. One of the ship's crew was holding the other end of the rope, and keeping an eye on Ryan.

Still, watching Ryan made me hold my breath.

Then he cut off eye contact, and was back to trying to figure out how best to reach the top of the wall. He moved slowly toward the top. His foot slipped, my breath caught, and Brooke released a tiny shriek.

Then Ryan regained his footing, eased up, touched the top, and shoved himself away from the wall.

The guys clapped and high-fived one another

like they were the ones who'd made it to the top. Ryan rappelled down and hit the ground. After an assistant helped him out of the harness, he strutted over to where we were standing.

"So, are you going to give it a go?" he asked, looking directly at me, giving the impression that everyone else was inconsequential.

"I thought I would," I responded.

"Have you ever climbed before?" he asked.

"No," I admitted.

"Don't try to go too fast, and don't reach too far," he suggested. "And if you get tired, just rappel back down."

"You make it sound so easy," I said with a grin.

"It's not easy, but it's not as difficult as real mountain climbing."

"Dude, you've climbed real mountains?" Cameron asked.

Ryan shifted his attention over to Cameron, as though he was amused by the question. "Yeah, I'm big into experiencing the outdoors."

"Cool."

Ryan turned back to me and smiled. "Now I'll watch you climb."

CHAPTER 16

I wasn't what I'd call nervous. The butterflies fluttering beneath my ribcage had nothing at all to do with a fear of falling flat on my butt. They had more to do with Ryan being nearby and watching me.

As I stood for the second time in as many days getting harnessed up, I wished that Ryan had headed off to do something else. I wasn't bothered by any of the other guys watching my ungainly clamber up the wall.

But I was very self-conscious about having Ryan watch me. Which was insane. What did I care if he was watching the way I moved?

I didn't care. Okay, I cared a little. I cared a lot.

He'd looked so terrific and confident scaling the wall, and I was already feeling weak in the knees, and I hadn't even begun the ascent yet. I felt like failing would not only be a disappointment to me, but to Ryan as well.

I'd taken such joy in his success that I was

hoping he'd feel the same way about mine.

I listened as Joe, the rock-climbing-wall guide, gave me some tips for the placement of my feet and hands. Then I folded my hands around the two different anchors on the wall, placed a foot on a foothold, lifted myself up, and placed the other foot on another foothold.

Now I just had to let go with one hand, and reach for another handhold. A lot easier-sounding that it felt.

I was only a few inches from the ground, and I was already experiencing major concern over falling and landing hard on my butt.

"Take a deep breath and ease up," Ryan said.

"I know." I really didn't, but I wasn't going to admit it.

"Come on, Lindsay, we're all waiting," Brooke said.

I growled, wishing I'd told her to go first. I wasn't going to let her pressure me into scaling the wall quickly, and possibly losing my perch. She would just have to wait.

"Don't rush it," Ryan said.

"We'll be here all day if she doesn't hurry," Brooke said.

"Then you shouldn't have brought your

harem," Ryan said.

"A harem is a group of females," Brooke pointed out.

"I was being sarcastic," Ryan said.

"Guys!" I snapped. "I'm trying to concentrate here."

My hands were getting damp, and I thought if I didn't speed things up a little, I was going to simply slide right off the wall. I inhaled deeply, released my right hand, and grabbed the next hold.

This was *so* much harder than it looked. What had I been thinking to even contemplate doing this?

But no way was I going to quit now that I'd started.

I began preparing to move my foot up to the next foothold. . . . Did it!

"That's it," Ryan encouraged. "Slow and steady."

It wasn't simply about finding a hold I could reach, and going for it. The trick was figuring out what I could easily reach that would put me in a good position to move up. And it wasn't as though I had a terrific view and could clearly envision the strategy. I was flat against the wall, which seriously limited what I could see.

I released my hold, snatched the next out-cropping, and pulled myself up. My arms were actually starting to quiver from the strain. Not good. Not good at all.

I moved up. Deep breath, deep breath. Reach up, grab, step up, pull, breathe, release, grab, pull . . .

Over and over.

Then I heard clapping, chanting, *Go, go, go* . . .

I looked up and thought, *Nearly there. I can do this. I can reach the top. I just have to —*

My foot slipped, my heart lurched, and my stomach felt as though it had dropped right to the ground, even though I was still clinging to the wall. I scrabbled my foot over the rugged sur-face until I found purchase.

And then I was breathing heavier than I'd ever breathed in my life. Shoot! That was close.

Even though I knew the rope would save me from smashing headfirst into the ground, I wasn't thrilled with the prospect of not reaching the top of this wall. It was a matter of pride.

"You're almost there!" Ryan yelled.

I was?

Cautiously I glanced up. The top didn't seem

that far away. Even more cautiously I gazed downward.

Wow! I'd climbed a lot higher than I had realized. Just one fake boulder at a time. It was so tempting to simply lunge for the top and be done with the climb, but after working so hard, I didn't want to lose anything that I'd gained.

So I became more cautious, and crept up inch by inch, trying to ignore all the noise that was coming from below me. I really appreciated everyone's enthusiasm, but I found it distracting as well. And I certainly didn't want to lose my grip or my footing when I'd put so much effort into getting to this point.

My muscles burned with the strain, but I knew I could do this. I absolutely could. I held my breath, released my hold, and grabbed the top of the wall. I glanced down, located the foothold I wanted to shoot for—

Got it!

I eased up—

And was at the top of the wall, breathing normally at last!

I released a triumphant shout and gazed around. I had a three-hundred-and-sixty-degree unfettered view of the ship and the ocean.

It was magnificent. So worth the effort of the climb. I really wished someone was up here with me to share the sight. No wonder Ryan had encouraged me. He'd seen it. He knew the reward. Even though he hadn't stayed up for as long as I had, knowing him, he'd probably climbed the wall a dozen times already.

With a shout of joy I began rappelling down the rock wall, the rope now serving as my anchor. My feet landed on the deck. The guy in charge helped me get out of the harness. My legs were trembling. It was a strange feeling to be on solid ground, and not to be worrying about losing my footing.

I kinda staggered over to the waiting area where Brooke and the guys were crowding around. I'd barely reached them when someone yanked me around.

I found myself in a lip lock that threatened to suck the air right out of me. I was going cross-eyed trying to figure out who was slobbering his spit all over me. I heard the distant din of shouts and yells . . .

And then I was free, tottering back, and staring incredulously at Shooter.

"Thought you deserved a kiss for reaching

the top," he announced, with a goofy grin on his face.

If I'd known his sloppy, wet kiss was the reward, I wasn't certain I would have tried so hard to reach the top. I didn't know what to say.

Everyone's attention suddenly turned away from me as Cameron moved up to be harnessed, and people wanted to offer him encouragement. I sank down to the ground.

Ryan crouched in front of me. "Thought I was going to have to call in a medical team to have that guy surgically removed."

I couldn't stop myself from grinning. "It wasn't that bad."

"Is he your new boyfriend?"

"No. Actually, until a minute ago, I thought he was all about Brooke."

"You know these guys are all players. They're going to say and do anything to get you into bed."

"I can handle it."

"If you say so."

It irritated me that he doubted me. I knew these guys were players. I was one as well.

"Ryan, you're not responsible for me."

"Look, I'm on this cruise because of you. So

174

I feel some responsibility."

"Well, don't. It was nice of Walter to want to make sure I have my own personal buddy, but it was totally unnecessary. I can take care of myself. And you're free to do"—I waved my hand—"whatever."

"I appreciate that."

I struggled back to my feet. "I need to get back to the guys."

"We're still on for tonight, right?" he asked.

"Yeah. I'll see you at eight."

I'd climbed to the top, and all he'd noticed was Shooter kissing me. I couldn't have been more disappointed.

"Hey, Lindsay?"

I looked back at him.

He grinned and gave me a thumbs up. "That was a hell of a climb."

CHAPTER 17

Tonight isn't a date.

I told myself that over and over as I changed from one outfit to another, unable to decide on exactly what I should wear to a *show* that wasn't a movie or a high-school play. It was a show like I saw advertised on TV in Vegas, or on Broadway, or any number of other stage productions. It was so not a date.

Walter had purchased the tickets, was trying to be nice, was trying to make sure that everyone had a good time. Since he saw me as his daughter now, and he'd brought Ryan along on the cruise, he thought hooking us up was the way to go. So tonight we'd be hooked.

I'd really planned to be totally casual after the wedding, to relax completely for the remainder of the cruise. But here I was dabbing on lip gloss, mascara, and eye shadow. I repainted my fingernails. I even applied a hot iron to my hair, making it straight and sleek, and oh-so-not casual.

I couldn't believe all the trouble I was going

to, or how tightly knotted my stomach was. I almost felt as though I was back on that stupid rock climbing wall reaching for that last hold that would allow me to see everything that surrounded me.

Only I felt as though I wasn't seeing anything. It was so difficult not being with anyone I shared a past with. I liked Brooke. She was fun, and she certainly did believe in bringing the party with her. I had a feeling she was one of those people who didn't like to be alone. Not for even a second.

Which was cool. I didn't have a problem with that attitude. But I hadn't been too pleased with Shooter snatching an unexpected kiss. I had a feeling that Brooke would have been okay with it. The guys were probably thinking Brooke and I were like two peas in a pod when we were really more like an apple and an orange. Not much in common except for the fact that we were both girls.

But that too was all right, I supposed. Although I was now wishing that I hadn't asked Ryan to get Brooke a ticket. A little time away from the constant party atmosphere might have been nice.

On the other hand I did want to make the very most of this cruise, and being off by myself limited the opportunities.

The knock on my door had me taking a deep breath and a final glance in the mirror. I was wearing a slinky, sparkly pink dress that I'd picked up cheaply, thinking that I'd probably never wear it, but that it would be nice to have, just in case.

And here I was wearing it with sandals. I hoped I didn't give the appearance of having dressed up for a date. *Because this is so not a date*, I repeated to myself for about the hundredth time.

I crossed the room, opened the door, and, after seeing him, wondered if Ryan thought maybe this *was* a date. He looked terrific. He was wearing a light blue button up shirt, and slacks.

"I hadn't planned to get this dressed up while on the cruise," he began, then shrugged. "But I figured for a *show* . . ."

His eye-rolling made me laugh. "Same here," I admitted.

"I think there's some sort of dress code," he said.

"I figured. We didn't have as many dress codes in high school as this cruise has." Some of the dining rooms required fancy clothes—men in dinner jackets, ladies in dresses. Needless to say I planned to avoid them.

"Yeah, it's kinda strange to be on vacation, and have to dress up. Are you ready?"

I tugged on the small purse hanging off my shoulder. "Have key, will travel."

He laughed at that. He had a really nice laugh. A deep timbre that echoed along the hallway.

"We'll be at Ocho Rios tomorrow," I said, like maybe he didn't know where we were going. "What are you going to do?"

"Hike. Climb a waterfall."

We got on the elevator, and he pressed the button for the deck we needed.

"Figure I'll be doing the same. That, and shopping."

"I could use another toe ring," he said with a grin.

I patted his arm. "We'll see. You could always go with us."

That invitation had come out before I thought about it. I held my breath, not sure if I wanted him there or not. But he shook his head.

"I'm not much into crowds."

"I'm not sure how crowded it'll be."

"I was talking about in general. I was referring to the increasing entourage that seems to follow wherever you and Brooke go."

"They're all nice guys."

"If you say so."

The elevator stopped and we stepped off. I really didn't want to talk about Brooke, or the guys, or how much I was missing my friends and would gladly swap everyone I'd met here for just one friend I'd known forever.

We walked along the corridor, heading for the Starlight Lounge, where the show was being held.

"Look, I'm sorry for ragging on your friends," Ryan said.

I glanced over at him. "They're not really my friends. They're just people to have fun with. Friends take awhile to make."

As we neared, I could see there was already quite a crowd of people waiting to get in.

"There you two are!"

I turned in the direction of the familiar voice, and there was Brooke in a tight little outfit that dipped a little too low at the neckline, revealing the fact she had a lot more to offer than I did. She'd colored the tips of her dark, spiked hair blue.

"I've been waiting forever," she said. She sidled up between us so that she was in the middle.

"What do you know about the show?" she asked.

"Glittery and sexy," Ryan offered.

"I'll be the judge of how sexy it is," she said.

Our seats weren't reserved, but we managed to get close to the front of the stage. Each row was a long bench, and every so often a round table was situated so people would have a place to put their drinks.

Even with the jostling around and finding a place to sit, Brooke never relinquished her claim on being between us.

Which I told myself was just fine. Ryan was a surrogate Walter, and I really didn't need or want that. So if Brooke wanted to sit between us, that was okay with me.

And Ryan certainly didn't seem to mind. As a matter of fact, he seemed to be warming up to Brooke quite a bit. They were laughing and talking as though I wasn't even there.

I was the one who'd thought to include Brooke, and here I was feeling like a third wheel on a bicycle. Or an unreachable handhold on a climbing wall.

I'd noticed before what a touchy-feely kind of person Brooke was, but it had never really bothered me until tonight. She was constantly touching Ryan's arm, his shoulder, his hand—like they were both an item.

I really shouldn't have cared, but I did. I'd invited her, and she was completely ignoring me so that she could flirt with Ryan.

If not for me, she wouldn't be rubbing her shoulder up against his. And of all the guys she'd introduced me to, and had gathered around us, the hottest guy I'd met so far was the one I'd first met: Ryan.

I thought it was a little ironic. If only he wasn't connected to Walter, maybe there could have been something between us.

Wishful thinking on my part. Sure, our paths kept crossing. He was fun to dance with. He had great wall climbing skills. And way too much advice to offer. But other than that one amazing kiss, he'd shown no real interest in me. I felt like I was about as exciting and attractive as an iguana.

Yet here he was laughing at everything Brooke said like she was a female Jerry Seinfeld.

Thank goodness the lights dimmed and the curtains were drawn back so I had something to focus on rather than the show going on beside me.

I felt rather than saw Brooke move nearer to me.

"Ryan is so hot," she whispered loudly, as music suddenly blasted through the theater. "I've convinced him to hang around with us tomorrow at Ocho Rios."

I looked over at her. "Really?"

She nodded enthusiastically and wiggled her eyebrows. "The more, the merrier."

Totally bummed I turned my attention back to the stage. Hadn't I invited Ryan first? Hadn't he said no, and offered a lame excuse about not wanting to be in a crowd?

Hadn't he warned me that Brooke was trouble?

And here he was accepting her invitation to spend time together at Ocho Rios—after declining mine?

Jerk. As soon as I thought it, I took it back. He wasn't a jerk. I'd told him from the beginning that I didn't want him hanging around and looking after me. So maybe he'd declined my invitation because he hadn't thought it was sincere. I was so confused where Ryan was concerned.

I tried to concentrate on the show. The fantastic costumes. The sparkles, the glitter, and the absolute breathtaking display of talent. The dancing, singing, and performances were unlike anything I'd ever seen.

It was one of those experiences that at any other time in my life I would have truly enjoyed, but I was having a little private pity party. Because I couldn't figure out what I really wanted with Ryan. If I was honest with myself, part of me wanted to spend time with him, but then another part of me wanted to complete all the items on my list—including losing my virginity.

Besides, I couldn't get over the feeling that Ryan saw me as nothing more than a friend, someone Walter had asked him to watch over, and so from time to time he felt as though he needed to touch base with me.

A waitress in a sequined costume, which left very little to the imagination, came to take our drink orders. Nudging Ryan a little, Brooke ordered a Sex on the Beach. I didn't even know if she knew what the drink was. I think she just wanted to be clever with her order, and to toss a hint Ryan's way. Maybe be a little sophisticated. I just thought she was being a little pathetic. I was getting seriously irritated with her constant flirtation.

I asked for a piña colada. Ryan wanted a beer.

After my experience of drinking champagne around Ryan, I decided to limit myself to one drink, and before it arrived, I checked to make sure that I was still holding onto my purse. I didn't want to go through the embarrassment of losing track of it again.

Once the drinks arrived, I glanced over at my table partners. Brooke was leaning against Ryan and talking. I sipped my drink, and concentrated on the show before me.

Time seemed to drag by. The music was lively and fun, but anytime there was a lull in sound, I would hear Brooke talking to Ryan or giggling with him.

Ryan and I had talked, but it had never been with the enthusiasm that he was now exhibiting with Brooke. It was like they were soul mates or something. I wanted to reach around, tap them both on the shoulder, and say, "Remember me?"

You'd think they were on a date or something.

When the final number came to a close, I was a bit sorry to see it end because it was spectacular. But I was also glad that I'd have the opportunity to get away from flirtatious Brooke. I really couldn't explain why it bothered me so much to see her flirting with Ryan. I was already so used to seeing her flirt with all the other guys that I would have thought it wouldn't have bothered me to see her with Ryan.

But it did.

To my relief we parted ways once we got outside the theater.

"See you guys tomorrow," Brooke announced.

Then she patted Ryan's shoulder, and gave him a wink before she turned on her heel and bounced away.

Ryan was incredibly quiet as we strolled to the elevator. He seemed to have a lot on his mind as we rode to our deck, and I couldn't quite think of anything to say. How could I compete with bubbly Brooke when I felt like fizzled-out champagne.

The elevator came to a stop and we got off.

"Does your friend ever stop talking?" Ryan finally asked.

I glanced over at him.

"You didn't seem to mind her talking with you. She said you agreed to go hiking with us tomorrow."

"It was more like being in shock at the unexpected silence when she asked, and not replying fast enough before she filled in the answer for me."

"So you don't want to go with us?"

"I wouldn't say that. I'm okay with the idea. I wasn't too keen on trudging up the waterfalls by myself, so her invitation to join you works for me."

Only it hadn't worked when I'd invited him. That really irked me. I reached into my purse for my key.

"Want to catch a bite to eat and a movie?"

I paused, and then very slowly lifted my gaze to Ryan. "What?"

"I know it sounds odd, but I'm craving something familiar. The show was great, the dancers were fantastic, but it's not really my thing. Right now, I'm craving a burger and a movie. There's a multiplex theater onboard and midnight showings. I don't care what we go see. I'll even sit through a chick flick."

It was crazy. To be having what was supposed to be the greatest vacation of my entire life, and to spend even a minute of it at a movie theater, something I could do any time, day or night, when I was home. Heck! I *worked* in a movie theater!

Why would I want to go to one when I was on vacation? Because I realized that it would give me a little time with Ryan without anyone else around. And although I thought any type of involvement with him might mean disaster down the road, tonight I wanted to be with him.

Smiling, I nodded. "Yeah. I'm all over that."

"Great. Give me five minutes to throw on some jeans—"

"I'll need ten."

"You got it."

Actually it only took me about eight to get out of my dress and into jeans, a red off-the-shoulder tank, and slides. I fluffed my fingers through my hair to loosen it up a bit, applied fresh lip gloss, and was ready to go.

Ryan was waiting in the hallway when I opened the door.

We located a diner where he ordered a loaded triple and cheese while I went with a junior. I couldn't figure out where he was going to put all that food this late at night. We shared onion rings and drank shakes.

I couldn't believe how good it all tasted.

"This is really insane," I said around an onion ring. "To have all these exotic restaurants and all this food I've never tasted before, and to be sitting here eating a burger."

"I agree," he said, just before he took a sip of his shake. "But, man, is it hitting the spot."

He took a bite of his burger, chewed for a while, dipped an onion ring into ketchup, and asked, "Is Brooke serious about any of those guys who are hanging around her?"

I looked at him. He was studying me while it appeared he was absently eating the onion ring.

"I don't think so." I almost added that she seemed to like to sample anything in jeans, but I was trying to be nice and not jealous.

"How 'bout you?" he asked.

"What about me?"

"Are you serious about any of those guys?"

"Not really. I mean, like I said, they're nice, and it's fun to have people to do things with, and I want this to be a special vacation."

"I'm down with that." He finished off his burger.

When we got to the theater, I selected what I was certain was a movie that would have lots of romance and girly-girly stuff. No action, no guns blazing, no blood, no gore.

True to his word Ryan didn't seem to mind. We made our way to the theater. It was more crowded than I expected it to be, but we managed to locate some seats about three-fourths of the way up. The lights were still on, and advertisements were flashing on the screen.

"Seems like on a cruise, you ought to be able to get away from the ads," he said quietly beside me.

"I should warn you," I whispered. "I don't talk during movies. It really bothers me when people do, like they're sitting in their own living rooms or something."

"I hear you."

I chuckled at that. "Wouldn't you rather hear the movie?"

He grinned. "Yeah."

The lights dimmed, and I settled more comfortably into my seat. Ryan was right. I was in the mood for something totally familiar, and sitting in a movie theater provided that experience. How strange that only a few days out, I was already missing home.

We watched the previews in silence. Then they gave way to the beginning of the movie. I felt Ryan moving toward me. I eased over toward him, certain he was going to whisper something about the previews or the movie, totally unprepared for what he did say.

"That first night when you said sleeping with a guy was on your list . . . you weren't really talking about *sleeping*, were you?"

My heart was pounding. I'd really hoped that either I hadn't really said what I'd thought I had or he'd not heard me. Still, I whispered, "No."

"Why would you put that on a list of things to do?"

I swallowed hard. Maybe it was the darkness of the theater that made it easier to confess, but I found myself revealing my reason. "Because it's something I've never done before."

"Don't do it, Lindsay. Not with any of those guys Brooke has wrapped around her finger. You deserve better than her cast-offs."

I didn't know if it was Ryan—a guy, a friend—talking, or Walter's godson who was supposed to watch out for me offering advice.

"Why do you care?" I asked in a low voice.

"Because I like you, and I don't want to see you get hurt."

He liked me. So what was I supposed to do now? Give up my quest to find the perfect guy to have a fling with? And what if that perfect guy was Ryan?

But it couldn't be. A fling with Ryan was totally out of the question. But could there be something more between us?

CHAPTER 18

I woke up the next morning, and contemplated the wisdom of keeping my head buried beneath the pillow.

Ryan "liked" me, but I didn't know if his interest went beyond being just a friend because as soon as the movie began, he started watching it as though he hadn't said anything incredibly enlightening. And I hadn't asked exactly what he meant because I wasn't sure how I'd feel about any answer he gave. I'd run different scenarios through my mind.

We had a fling, parted ways, felt awkward every time our paths crossed in the future.

We had a fling, and when the cruise ended, we didn't part ways. What were the odds of that happening?

He'd told us that first night that he'd broken up with his girlfriend. What if he was like Brooke, looking to forget someone?

He didn't seem to be, but what did I know?

Did I want to risk getting involved with

Walter's godson? I simply didn't know. Mostly because I was scared. I'd never been in a serious relationship before, and it frightened me to think of how much it might hurt if things didn't work out. A fling was safer. No commitment. No expectations beyond the fling.

But suddenly the idea didn't seem as appealing. I just didn't know what to do except to continue on, and see what today brought my way.

I'd watched a special on TV about kissing, and about how kissing was really nature's chance to get close enough to sniff the other person, and determine if the chemistry was right. It wasn't the most romantic thing I'd ever heard, but I was beginning to think that I needed to apply myself more diligently to that item on my list that said "Kiss lots of cute guys."

I threw off the covers, scrambled out of bed, crossed the cabin, slid open the glass door, and stepped onto the balcony. I raised my arms above my head, and stretched to one side, then the other.

It was a glorious morning, the island visible in the distance. I was supposed to meet with Brooke soon—and who knew how many guys. Today was the day for a personality change. Today I would find Mr. Perfect-for-One-Night.

I spun on my heel and froze as my gaze fell on Ryan, standing on his balcony watching me.

"How long have you been there?" I asked.

"Longer than you."

He sipped from a mug, and I could smell the aroma of coffee now that I was aware that he was here.

I stepped toward the low wall that separated our balconies. "Are you still planning to hang around with us today?"

"No reason not to. Is there?"

"No reason at all."

I wanted to move away from him, but at the same time I wanted to stay where I was. What if he was the one? What if he wasn't? "I guess I need to get ready."

"I'll meet you in the hallway."

I went back inside and got dressed. Cargo shorts, tank, old tennis shoes. I'd read the brochure on Dunn's River Falls and knew that while the temptation was to go barefoot over the slippery rocks, shoes were recommended. As a matter of fact, once I'd known that I'd be on this cruise, I'd spent a good deal of time planning everything so that it would become the best vacation ever.

Just goes to show that sometimes the best-laid plans don't work out. But we were still in the early stages of the cruise, and I had several more days and nights to see to it that I accomplished my goals.

After settling a visor onto my head, I pulled on matching wristbands. I stuffed a beach towel, suntan lotion, some snacks and a bottle of water from the minibar, and a romance novel into my backpack, along with other essentials. We'd be gone most of the day. Then this evening there would be more partying in the various clubs that dotted the town.

I hitched my backpack onto my shoulder, and headed out the door. Ryan was waiting in the hallway with his own backpack slung over his shoulder. Like me, he was wearing scruffy-looking tennis shoes.

"Let's go," I ordered.

As Ryan and I came on deck, the ship was docking at the pier. We were greeted by white sands and palm trees. An island paradise.

"There you are!"

Brooke rushed up to us and grabbed my arm. "I've hooked us up with Jake."

"Jake?"

"He's an activities director, and he's going to lead one of the trips to Dunn's River Falls. Come on. We'll be leaving soon."

I followed her through the crowd, with Ryan on my heels.

"Wonder why she didn't get us into a group with a Jane or a Joan or a Josie?" he asked quietly behind me.

Because that wasn't Brooke's style. I was really beginning to feel quite flattered that she'd ever approached me, and was including me in her activities.

Jake was a cutie, not much older than us. Or at least he didn't look much older. The usual suspects—Chad, Shooter, Marc, Michael, Cameron, David—were gathered around him. There were also two girls who Brooke introduced as Donna and Cathy, although she didn't seem too impressed with them.

"They were like leeches, sucking up to Jake so they could be part of his group," Brooke whispered beside me.

Ironically I figured she'd been just as leechy.

"I was checking out all the activity directors this morning," she continued, "and Jake is definitely the cutest. No ring on his finger."

Jake clapped his hands to get everyone's attention. He had short-cropped blond hair and green eyes. He looked strangely out of place, dressed in his *Enchantment* uniform polo, instead of an old T-shirt like the rest of us.

"Okay, guys, I'm Jake. I'll be your activity director today. I need you to very quickly give me your first names."

We all gave him our names, which I figured was probably a complete waste of time. How was he going to remember us all?

"Okay," he continued once we finished the introductions. "We're going to walk through a government building and into the town. People are going to be trying to sell stuff to you. But we're on a schedule this morning, so don't stop to make any purchases. Go straight to the mini-vans. Seven to a van. Our group will take two.

"When we get to the falls, I'll take your cameras. The rest of your stuff we'll lock in the van. The falls are slippery, so you don't want to be carrying anything. If you have water shoes, you'll want to put them on. Any questions?"

Brooke raised her hand.

"Yes, ma'am?"

"Are you married?"

He laughed. "No, miss. Any other questions?"

Everyone looked around at everyone else silently. I did have water shoes in my backpack. I'd put them on at the falls.

"Did you hear him?" Brooke asked me. "He called me 'miss.' How cute was that?"

Jake clapped his hands again and smiled broadly. "All right then. Let's rock!"

It was interesting walking into town. It was a bustling array of people. Musicians were playing on homemade steel drums. Hats and pots sat at their feet. As we walked by, we tossed some money into the containers. The people looked terribly poor.

Here we were with no cares in the world, and these people were desperate to sell us things.

A woman touched my arm. "Beautiful lady, let me make you more beautiful."

Her accent was very English. She wanted to braid my hair. I gave her a smile and promised, "This afternoon."

I understood now why Jake had warned us that we wouldn't have time to do any browsing or shopping to begin with. I really wanted to stop and have my hair braided with the beads.

Especially when all the vendors kept calling me "beautiful lady."

We crowded onto the minivan. Brooke, Ryan, and I were in one van along with a couple of the other guys and Jake. As the van began rolling, Jake turned in his seat. I was sitting right behind him.

He stood slightly and addressed the crowd. "Having a good cruise?"

He received an abundance of enthusiastic responses. "Tonight is the singles meet on the Starlight deck. I want to see you guys there. Who's going snorkeling when we hit the Grand Cayman?"

Another round of abundant yes's greeted him.

"Cool! Hook up with me in the morning, and I'll give you a quick lesson when we hit the beach."

He settled back in his seat, but at an angle so he was able to look at me. "Lindsay, right?"

I smiled. "Right. I'm surprised you remembered."

"I'm good with names." He shifted a bit so he was leaning a little over his seat and was closer to me. "So, Lindsay, where are you from?"

CHAPTER 19

We stood on the sandy beach, looking at the breathtaking falls. The water cascaded over tiers of smooth rock to fall into the Caribbean Sea. They went about six hundred feet up from where we stood, and we couldn't see the top because it wasn't a straight waterfall. It was more like a shallow river rushing down the side of a mountain. Hence it's name. Dunn's River Falls.

"Pictures! Pictures!" Brooke cried.

As soon as we'd clambered out of the van, we'd handed our cameras to Jake. Because he was more experienced climbing the falls, he was going to take all the pictures so we could concentrate more on hiking up the slippery slope.

Brooke grabbed my arm, and dragged me into the ice cold oceanic water at the base of the falls. Then we leaned against a boulder while the water rushed around us and flowed into the Caribbean. Typical tourist pose, standing where the river and the ocean met.

Jake took a camera out of the bag he was

holding, and began snapping photos. Then he took out another camera. Another photo. He ran through the gamut of cameras, and had everyone posing for pictures.

Hamming it up. Group photos, single photos. It was obvious he loved what he was doing. He had us laughing and goofing around.

Ryan seemed amused by the whole photo shoot, and he even periodically stepped into a group to be photographed, which surprised the heck out of me. I was even more surprised that Brooke wasn't giving him gobs of special attention today, but I was learning that when guys were in abundance, Brookes affections were unpredictable.

I didn't want to think about her possibly disappearing with Ryan, like she had with David our first night hanging out.

Although it was morning I could tell that it was going to be a warm day. The cold water from the falls was going to feel terrific by day's end.

Jake put the cameras away. Then he climbed onto a rock, and began explaining how to safely scale the waterfall.

Six hundred feet up.

I thought about the climb I'd done the day

before. Twenty-five feet, and I was feeling just a tad sore in my arms and legs. Six hundred feet, even for someone who was in shape, was bound to be a challenge. I focused my attention completely on Jake.

"You can walk up the trail next to the falls," he said. "But if you're physically able, I encourage you to actually walk up the falls. It's an awesome experience. If you're really in great shape, you can walk up alone. But I recommend that you do it as part of a chain. We'll all hold hands, support one another, and make it a fun hike. So those of you who want to go up with me, let's form a single line and grab hands."

Brooke and I had been standing together to have our pictures taken, but it was obvious that she didn't want to travel up the slippery slope holding my hand. And truthfully I didn't want to hold hers either.

She made a rather dramatic attempt to get first in line, which put her in position to hold hands with Jake.

I was looking around for Ryan, not certain why he was my first choice. Suddenly I realized that he was there, standing beside me. I didn't know why I felt relief.

"Ryan!"

Brooke was calling to him. I sorta hoped he'd ignore her, but I quickly realized as he started toward her that he had no plans to do that. Then he reached back, grabbed my hand, and pulled me along.

"It'll be more fun and probably safer at the front," he said.

"I don't need safe," I retorted. Honestly, the guy didn't constantly have to look after me. I wanted a little danger.

We got into position, and I realized that Shooter and Cameron had scrambled over the rocks to take up their positions behind us.

"Dude!"

I turned in time to see Cameron give Shooter a little push.

"I was here first," Cameron said.

"Yeah, but I kissed her," Shooter said.

Cameron turned quickly and planted a kiss on my mouth before I could protest. His teeth hit mine with a *clack*.

"Dibs!" he said.

"You guys are *so* immature," Brooke said.

She was now holding Ryan's hand, and waiting for Jake to take hold of hers. I slipped my hand into Ryan's free one, because truthfully, Ryan was much more buff. And I figured if anyone could make sure I didn't slip down this wall of a mountain that we were going to climb, it would be Ryan.

Just to stop the arguing I grabbed Cameron's hand.

"I met Cameron first," I explained with an apologetic smile at Shooter. I'd take a clacking kisser over a slobbering one any day.

Shooter took the news with a puppy-dog look, before shrugging his shoulders. He walked off, stopped beside Cathy, and took her hand.

Cameron grinned at me. "It's you and me, babe."

"Wasn't that an old rock song?" Ryan asked.

I wasn't sure if it was or not. I only knew that if Cameron came for me again with another kiss in mind, I was ducking.

Taking the lead, Jake grabbed Brooke's hand and started up the cascading falls.

Dunn's River Falls is a Jamaican national treasure. As our human chain made its way up the falls, I was in awe of the majesty surrounding me. The water cascaded swiftly over rocks that went up a mountainside. Climbing the falls meant climbing the mountain. Lush green foliage was everywhere. Exotic ferns, orchids, lilies, palms, bamboo, and other trees and flowers whose names I didn't know.

Whenever I thought tropical paradise, I thought of a place like this. The water rushed over our feet as we climbed higher. I wasn't certain if I was growing accustomed to it or if the water was becoming warmer.

Every now and then I slipped, and it was a constant battle to move against the water flowing past. But always Ryan was there holding firm. I was really grateful that he was walking ahead of me.

He was surefooted. Sometimes when the step up was steep, he pulled me up. Then he'd release his hold on me and give Cameron a hand.

And sometimes Jake would stop and give everyone a hand at a really difficult crossing.

He'd always wink at me. "How you holding up?" he'd ask.

"Just great."

I didn't think he was giving me any special attention. I figured it was just part of his job to make sure that everyone was doing all right, and having a good time.

Ryan and I, along with the human chain, trudged up the side of the mountain. I didn't know how his hand stayed so warm when the water rushing past us often seemed icy cold. But, then, it was only the water that was really cold. The air was warm and moist—a direct contrast to the water.

The climb was invigorating and exciting, and unlike anything I'd ever experienced. The higher we went, the more tired I was. I'd always thought I was in shape, but I was panting, my legs ached, and my feet grew heavier. I was beginning to wonder if I'd have the strength or endurance to make it to the top.

"We're going to take a rest up here!" Jake called down.

Thank goodness! was all I seemed capable of thinking.

Just a few more steps up, and we reached a pool of green water.

"Hold your nose!" Ryan yelled.

Before I could react, he'd wrapped his arms around me, and we were falling backward into the icy water.

CHAPTER 20

It was cold, cold, cold!

I came up out of the water shrieking and soaked and laughing so hard my ribs ached.

Ryan was laughing too and apparently he'd started a trend because a couple of the guys who'd been behind us grabbed Cathy and Donna, and carried them into the pool. Even Brooke found herself dunked a couple of times.

I scooted over to the edge of the pool. I quickly grew accustomed to the water's temperature. It didn't seem nearly as cold as I'd thought it was at first.

And now that I was here, I wanted to stay for a while. Just stay and relax and let my muscles unwind.

Jake crouched at the edge of the pool, his smile bright. "We're about halfway up the falls," he said.

Beside me, Brooke groaned. "You didn't say it would be so hard."

"You can go up on the trail if you need to," Jake said.

Brooke gave him a look that said she wasn't taking that route unless he was. Then she looked at me. "Are you interested in doing the trail?"

"Not really. I can walk trails at home."

"I guess once we rest for a while, it won't seem so hard," she said.

Jake turned from guide into photographer, and began taking pictures again, using everyone's camera.

"How many times have you taken this trek?" I asked him.

"About a hundred. It never grows old."

"It's so beautiful here," I said.

"Maybe I'll stay, and you can pick me up on the way back down," Brooke muttered.

"You're nuts," Ryan said. "This is great, working our way up the mountain."

"You're just saying that because you're sandwiched between two girls," Brooke said.

Ryan grinned before disappearing beneath the water.

Brooke edged closer to me. "I really like him," she whispered.

"What about all the other guys?" I asked.

"What about them?"

"You invited them to join us."

"That doesn't mean that I have to settle for

one of *them*." She shrugged. "Besides, I invited Ryan too."

"I invited him first."

"He didn't mention that to me."

I didn't know what to say, but I knew I didn't want to fight over Ryan. I rolled my shoulder. "It doesn't matter. He's here. All the guys we've met are here. So let's have fun."

Ryan came up out of the water a short distance away. He stood, flicked back his wet hair, and walked toward us, arms outstretched. "Let's go!"

I was really hoping that Brooke wouldn't put her hand in his, but she did. And then I thought how silly it was to care. I mean, he'd never given any indication that he liked me as more than a friend. Practically tossing me into the river was something that you'd do with your kid sister or your good pal.

He hadn't dunked Brooke, and he was following behind her now. I was okay with that. I really was. Or at least I tried to convince myself that I was.

Cameron came up beside me, and with a self-conscious grin, took my hand.

"This is kinda like a school field trip where you have to stay with your buddy," he said.

I slipped, fell to a knee, fought to ignore the sharp pain, and looked up at him. "Not really. If I wasn't holding onto you guys, I'd be slipping and sliding all the way down the falls."

He and Ryan pulled me back to my feet.

We slowly and laboriously worked our way over the falls. Jake pointed out various plants and some wildlife from time to time.

Every now and then, someone would break off from the group, and at Jake's direction take a steeper route. I considered trying the more challenging path, but in the end I followed the somewhat easier one. Although easier is a relative term, and it wasn't really easy.

I knew I'd be sore the next day. But a good kind of sore. Aching muscles that had been pushed to the limit. And a bruised knee.

The higher we went, the more often Brooke lost her balance. I was beginning to think she did it on purpose just to have Ryan's attention. And maybe Jake's as well. Every time she slipped, they both helped her up.

They were being gentlemen. Still, I didn't much like it.

Once she'd apologized for being so clumsy, we'd start up the trail again. Ryan would look back at me to take my hand.

"You okay?" he asked.

I beamed at him. "Fine."

At one point, Cameron leaned toward me and asked, "Is he your ex-boyfriend?"

I shook my head. "Friend of the family."

Which was absolutely true. He was Walter's godson and Walter was my stepdad so in a roundabout way, Ryan was a friend of the family. I'd never put it all together like that before, and it sorta made my feelings toward him shift.

It wasn't that he was baby-sitting me or watching me as a favor to Walter. He was here because he was a friend of the family.

I should be nicer. Take Brooke's lead, and invite him to join us on things. Even though he said no to me and yes to Brooke—maybe if I was more enthusiastic with my invitations . . .

I didn't know where the time went, but suddenly we were standing at the top of the falls, looking down on where we'd come from. It was so gorgeous.

Paradise.

"I think I could stay here forever," I said to no one in particular.

"The coming and going is too much work," Brooke said.

I rolled my eyes, and wondered why today of all days, she had to be such a whiner.

Ryan slung his arm around my shoulder. "I'm with you. It's beautiful up here."

Brooke wandered closer, and nudged herself up under Ryan's free arm. "Hey, Jake!" she yelled. "Take a picture."

Jake began sorting through all the cameras he was carrying.

"That one!" Brooke yelled.

He lifted the camera. I leaned in closer to Ryan, and smiled. Jake pointed.

"Say 'paradise.'"

"Paradise!" we yelled.

I eased out from beneath Ryan's arm, and began strolling around, looking at the vegetation, studying the rocks, just simply enjoying this haven. The islands held such appeal. Maybe when I was finished with college, I'd return to the Caribbean to live and work. Or maybe I'd simply take another vacation here.

"What are you thinking?" Ryan asked quietly.

I glanced over my shoulder. I hadn't realized that he'd followed me.

"I was thinking how peaceful it all is. I think this is definitely my favorite spot so far."

Ryan was studying me, and I thought maybe

there was something he wanted to say, but then Brooke was tugging on his hand.

"Come on, we're heading back down," she said. "Jake promised a party at the bottom of the falls."

I was enjoying the party up here. Sure, it was a different kind of music, nature's lullaby, but it was soothing and calming.

"So are you ready to head down?"

It was Cameron, my faithful companion. I guess he'd gotten dibs on me again—this time without the kiss.

"Sure," I said. I slipped my arm through the crook of his elbow.

Going down the falls was a little different. We followed the trail beside the falls. It allowed us to view the falls from a completely different perspective, looking at everything from where we'd climbed up.

I really did love this place.

Until I caught sight of Brooke and Ryan, off to the side, almost hidden by the dense green foliage. . . .

Kissing.

CHAPTER 21

"I'm sorry to bother you, but I'm new on this ship. Could you give me the directions to your cabin?"

I stared at the guy who I was certain thought he'd had an original come-on line. It was only the fifth time I'd heard it in less than an hour.

I was on the Starlight deck where the singles' meet was taking place, wondering why guys thought corny pickup lines were the way to go. Every time I thought I'd heard them all, along came a guy with another one.

The party was actually fun, and the guys all seemed pretty harmless. Jake kept walking around, keeping an eye on things, making sure people were mingling, and having fun.

But I still hadn't figured out exactly how to respond when a guy was standing before me with a goofy grin and hope in his eyes.

"I have a terrible sense of direction," I told him.

He walked away, and I overheard him using

the same line on another girl who was standing nearby.

"That was a clever comeback," someone said quietly behind me.

I turned around and there was Jake. I shrugged. "I didn't want to hurt his feelings."

"Is this your first singles' event?"

"Yeah. Somehow I missed the others."

"Well, a lot of people travel alone. I try to hook them up so they have a good time." He angled his head thoughtfully. "Only I didn't realize you were alone. I thought you were with Ryan."

I shook my head. "We hang out together now and then, but we're not together."

Any thoughts I'd had that we might end up together had totally disappeared when I'd spotted Ryan kissing Brooke. Worst of all was the realization of how much it had hurt.

During the remainder of the afternoon, it had been difficult to pretend that I hadn't seen them, that the sight of them hadn't been like a punch to the gut. But somehow I managed.

After we had walked back down the falls, the whole gang had spent some time on the beach soaking up the late-afternoon sunshine. We'd eaten dinner at a club, and listened to reggae music. Then we'd returned to the ship.

Brooke and Ryan hadn't done any more kissing. At least not that I'd seen. Brooke had been like a tour director, telling us where to go and what to do. Ryan had been pretty quiet.

I was confused by my reaction to seeing them, and totally bummed by how connected they seemed to be. Even though I knew I had no right to be.

Brooke had asked me if I had an interest in Ryan. I'd told her no—which had made Ryan available to her. I couldn't have it both ways, and I knew it. If I wasn't claiming a guy then Brooke was free to pursue him. I couldn't be upset, because she'd done exactly that: pursued Ryan. Brooke was my buddy for the trip. Ryan had really shown no acute interest in me. Yes, we hung out at the movies and the show, and he'd spent today with us, but I wasn't the main attraction.

Apparently Brooke was.

I'd been so busy palling around with both Brooke and Ryan that I was in danger of not reaching my ultimate goal: finding a guy to be alone with.

"Are you going snorkeling tomorrow?" Jake asked.

I'd been so lost in my morose thoughts that I'd almost forgotten that he was there.

"Definitely."

"Glad to hear it." He glanced around, before looking back at me. "Listen, I need to get some more people to start dancing. Would you mind being my partner to start off with?"

"Beats standing here listening to corny pickup lines."

"You think they're corny, huh?"

"Pretty much, yeah."

"You know we give all the guys a little card with 'lines guaranteed to work' written on it when they come onboard the ship."

I laughed. "Well, the lines aren't working."

"They're not?"

"No." I gave him a hard look. "You don't really give out cards, do you?"

"Nah. Do you think we should?"

"Yeah, maybe. You wouldn't believe some of the things I've heard so far tonight."

"And not a single one worked on you?"

"Not so far."

"That's where you're wrong," he said, taking my hand. "Mine did."

Talk about smooth!

I hadn't even realized he'd been coming on to me. Even as he led me to the middle of the deck, and urged other couples to follow us—he'd point to a guy, then a girl, nod, and put his fingers together—I wasn't convinced that he was really making a move on me.

He was cruise ship personnel, and I figured he wasn't supposed to get serious with the passengers. He was just making me feel good. That was his job.

I'd even heard that for older couples there were guys on the ships known as "escorts," whose job it was to spend time with lonely older women—not in a sexual way. Just as companions. Always being sure they had someone to dance with.

It occurred to me that Jake might be fulfilling that role now. Maybe he'd been feeling sorry for me. Maybe like Ryan he had this need to watch out for me, to make sure I had a good time.

As we started to dance, he gave me a sincere smile and a wink. I found myself wishing that he wasn't part of the cruise ship, that he was a passenger, and that something could happen between us. I was fairly certain, though, that his getting involved with me or anyone else onboard could cost him his job.

So I kept things light. I simply enjoyed dancing with him. And I tried not to be too disappointed when he worked us to the edge of the crowd, grabbed a guy's arm, made quick introductions, and left me dancing with Roger.

Roger was nice, in a gangly sort of way. His dancing style reminding me of a scarecrow caught in a tornado.

"So where are you from?" Roger asked.

I told him. He was from Houston.

When the music stopped, neither one of us really knew what else to say. Apparently he'd flunked the flirtation quiz too.

"Hey, Roger." It was Jake, and he had a girl in tow. "This is Angela, and she's had her eye on you all night. Would you dance the next one with her?"

While Roger and Angela were getting to know each other, Jake took my arm and walked me away from the group.

"Let me get you something to drink," he offered.

He led me to the bar that they'd set up on the deck, and ordered me a frozen strawberry daiquiri and a water for himself. Once we had our drinks he led me to the railing, away from the crowds.

"Sorry about hooking you up with Roger, but if I spend too much time with you, I'll get reprimanded."

"It's okay. Roger was fun."

"Do you like him better than you like me? Because if you do—"

"Oh, no," I blurted out. "I just wanted you to know that it was okay. I understand. You're working."

"Yeah, I am. Which can be a pain when I meet a girl that I really like."

I felt my heart do a little dance along my ribs, in rhythm with the music filling the Starlight deck.

"Think there's any chance of anything happening between us if you have to share me with the others?" he asked.

I nodded, feeling tongue-tied and awkward, and wishing for the millionth time I'd studied that darn flirtation quiz better.

"Cool. Tomorrow during the snorkeling excursion, there won't be so many watchful eyes. Maybe we can get some time alone. I'd really like to get to know you better, Lindsay."

"I'd like that," I said. "Having some time alone."

He winked at me. "Count on it then. Right now I've got to make sure these guys are partying more." He squeezed my hand. "But tomorrow, I'll find some time for us."

The next morning I began my day by blading along the jogging trail before most people were up and about. The rhythm of my blades was calming, and helped me put things into perspective.

And how could anyone stay uptight or bummed out when on a cruise? The sun easing over the horizon and reflecting off the water was inspiring. It made me feel like I could do anything, accomplish any goal.

Even finding Mr. Perfect-for-One-Night didn't seem quite so daunting. Especially when I had Jake's attention.

Actually I'd been hoping that I'd run into him this morning. He was really nice and caring. Trying to make sure that everyone had a good time.

And I certainly enjoyed being with him. Maybe he was the one I'd been looking for all along.

I rounded a corner that I'd gone past at least half a dozen times already, and I nearly tripped over my own feet at the sight of Brooke caught in another lip lock.

Only this time she wasn't with Ryan. She was with Cameron. They broke apart. She tossed her head back, and laughed—her familiar dramatic pose.

Then she spotted me, waved, patted Cameron on the shoulder, and walked toward the jogging track. I came to a stop.

"Geez, you're out early this morning," she said.

I looked past her to where Cameron had been. "So are you."

"I spent the night with Cam. He was walking me back to my cabin."

I hardly knew what to say. "But yesterday you were hitting on Ryan—"

"He is so boring."

"Ryan is boring?" I'd never found him boring. What in the world was she going on about?

"Definitely," she said. "No chemistry whatsoever."

No chemistry? But what about what I'd felt when Ryan had kissed me when we were parasailing? I'd definitely felt chemistry and electricity.

Brooke obviously thought Cameron had chemistry, but when he'd kissed me . . .

Well, he'd done nothing for me. Not even a up-on-my-toes kind of feeling. I guess it just went to prove that kissing was subjective, and what one person liked, another didn't.

"Want to grab some breakfast?" Brooke asked.

"Sure. Let me get my shoes."

I rolled over to where I'd left my backpack and shoes; I'd figured both were relatively safe on the bench. Everything important I'd carried with me. But shoes and an empty backpack— who'd really want them?

I sat on the bench, removed the Rollerblades, stuffed them into my backpack, and slipped on my slides. Then I joined Brooke.

We had breakfast at a little corner bakery kind of café. I had a cream cheese Danish and hot green tea, while she had a blueberry muffin and an espresso.

"So how did you and Cameron hook up?" I asked, genuinely curious. She'd still been snuggling against Ryan when we'd returned to the ship just yesterday evening.

"When we got back to the ship, you took off

for parts unknown," she said. "The rest of us hit the club. Ryan didn't stay long. Cameron did."

"So it's not like love," I said.

"No, not at all. Are you looking for love, Lindsay?"

I didn't know why her question felt like a blow to the midsection. I wasn't looking for love. Was I?

I decided to confess. "I was sorta hoping for a shipboard romance."

"So why aren't you having one? We've met lots of guys."

"But none have really been Mr. Right."

She rolled her eyes. "Mr. Right is long-term. You have to lower your standards if you want to get hot and heavy with a guy really fast."

"Is that what you did?" I asked. "Lowered your standards?"

She laughed. "I've never had high standards. Love 'em and leave 'em, and never get hurt."

"But you did get hurt. What about the guy you just broke up with?"

"I don't want to talk about him. I'm here to help you get it on with someone."

"I think I can find someone without your help."

"Who has been the one to find us all the guys? I'm a guy magnet," she said.

"Yeah, but the guys you find don't really do anything for me."

"What about Chad? You found him on your own."

"He's too much into guzzling beer. Everything is a competition with him. I don't want to feel like I'm a prize."

"Lindsay, Lindsay, you really don't get the casual dating scene."

I dumped a packet of sugar into my tea, and stirred it to give myself something to do while I thought of what I should say. Brooke wasn't my best bud, but she was the closest thing I had to a friend on this cruise.

"Brooke, I've never slept with a guy."

She gave me this incredulous look. "You slept with Ryan."

It was embarrassing to admit, but I'd gone this far. "All we did was sleep."

Her mouth dropped open, and she flopped back against her chair. "You mean, you only slept, like with your eyes closed, and snores, and dreams—"

"Right. It's a long story, but the first night

when I got back to my cabin I didn't have my key with me. It was late, Ryan and I were a little drunk, and I sort of fell asleep in his room."

"He doesn't kiss like he's gay."

I laughed at the absurdity of her response. "He's not gay."

"Then why did he only sleep with you?"

"He's just not attracted to me."

She looked completely baffled. "That makes no sense."

"It doesn't matter," I said hastily. "The point in my telling you all this is so you'll realize that I need someone special. I'm not opposed to lowering my standards some, but I can't lower them all the way, because I need someone special. For me, it'll be the first time."

"I'll say." She sat up straighter. "We need to go on a guy-hunting expedition."

"No, we don't. I may have found someone," I confessed.

She raised her eyebrows at that. "Really?"

"Jake."

"The activities director?"

I nodded. "I went to that singles' meet he had last night. He introduced me to several guys, but it was like he was hoping I wouldn't really be into any of them. It was like he was doing his job, but only because it was his job."

"That's interesting. He's cute."

"I think so."

"So what are the plans for today?"

"We'll be arriving at the Grand Cayman soon. We'll go snorkeling."

"Oh, right." She scrunched up her face. "Another water thing."

"Brooke, we're on a ship, in the middle of the ocean, heading for an island. Yes, another water thing."

"It's just that it's a total waste of time to style your hair or do your makeup, because the wind, the sand, and the water screw it all up. Too bad we don't have time to get you a tattoo, something to make you seem mysterious."

Was that the reason that I didn't have guys hanging all over me? Because I didn't have a tattoo?

Although truthfully I'd had several guys express an interest. I'd even had four of them kiss me. It's just that none of them really did anything for me.

Except Ryan, who wasn't interested.

"I don't think a tattoo is the secret," I told her.

"It doesn't hurt. Are you sure you don't want to get your tongue pierced?"

"I'm sure."

She scowled. "Where's your sense of adventure?"

"I keep it right next door to my common sense."

"Dullsville." She stood and began gathering her trash. "Don't worry. I'll take care of it."

I stood as well. "Brooke, don't. I've got a handle on the situation, and Jake doesn't need any prompting. He liked me just fine last night."

"But 'just fine' doesn't get a guy into your bed."

"I'm not even sure he's allowed to do that sort of thing with passengers. As a matter of fact I'm pretty sure he's not."

She grinned. "Which means he must be a rule breaker."

She started to walk off, and I grabbed her arm. "Brooke, please, don't do *anything*."

She released a sigh of frustration. "Oh, all right. But if you decide that you want help, don't hesitate to let me know. I have a way with guys."

"So I noticed."

"I can tell from looking at a guy if he's any

good in the sack or not."

"How can you tell?" I asked, not even trying to hide the skepticism in my voice.

"It's all in their eyes. Bedroom eyes, I call it. It's just a hot, sultry look. Guys with blue eyes come by it naturally. All the others have to work at it."

"So, is Jake good?" I asked, even though I didn't believe she had any psychic abilities or anything.

"Oh, definitely. And before this cruise is over, you'll know for sure."

CHAPTER 23

Jake's excursion group was the same group that he'd had for the falls. I had sorta hoped that Ryan wouldn't show up, because I didn't think I'd feel comfortable flirting with Jake if Ryan was near enough to watch. I thought he might be judging my actions, might tell me as he had at the movies that I'd simply found another guy that it was best to ignore.

But Ryan did show up in a swimsuit and a tank top. I was still feeling unexplainably hurt that he'd kissed Brooke, but my good manners forced me to at least acknowledge Ryan's arrival with a nod of my head. And he really had no reason not to kiss Brooke. I'd told him repeatedly that he didn't need to hang around me.

I was standing near Jake when I spotted Ryan talking with one of the girls from yesterday. Cathy or something. And that was good. If Ryan was busy with her, he wouldn't notice that Jake was giving any attention to me.

Jake took us to a local diving shop so we

could either rent or purchase our equipment. I was looking over the rental gear when I felt a familiar presence behind me.

"You should go ahead and buy what you need," Ryan said. "You'll get hooked."

I glanced down and noticed that he was carrying a netted bag that already had equipment in it. I assumed he'd brought it with him.

"I suppose you've snorkeled before."

"Yeah. I've done a little diving, too. But I only dive when I'm with someone who is experienced, and knows what he's doing. I have my doubts about Jake on either score."

"Ouch!" I said, and followed it with an incredulous laugh. "That's a little harsh, isn't it?"

"Maybe. I saw him hitting on you at the singles' meet last night."

"You were there?"

"For a while. I think he's interested in giving you some private lessons while we're here," he said.

"And that's a problem because? . . ." I shook my head. "Look, Ryan, I'm cool, okay? You don't have to watch out for me."

"Walter—"

"I know Walter brought you along to keep

me company, but I'm fine by myself. Honestly. Go have some fun." I leaned toward him. "Besides, I didn't give you any advice about Brooke."

His eyes widened. "Brooke?"

"I spotted you and her yesterday, on the way down the falls. I'm cool with it if you're interested in her."

"For your information I'm not interested in her. She came on to me. She reminded me of an octopus."

"Yeah, you really looked like you didn't want to be wrapped in her arms."

"Look, Lindsay—"

"Don't worry about me, Ryan. I'm a big girl. I can take care of myself."

With that I skirted around him, and went in search of some equipment to buy because I figured Ryan was probably right. I would want to snorkel more than once, and we might even be able to get some snorkeling time in when we got to Cozumel.

I was looking at masks when Jake came over.

"Try this one on," he said.

I tried it on and looked at him. It seemed fine to me, but then I really wasn't sure what I was looking for.

"What do you think?" I asked, and thought I sounded a little funny breathing through my mouth while I talked.

"You want a snug fit so the water can't get in. Nothing is more irritating than having your mask fill up with water."

He slowly trailed his finger around the edge of my mask, around my face. The whole time he kept his gaze anchored on mine.

"You've got killer eyes, you know that?" he finally said.

I grinned. "That was one of the come-on lines from last night. I think it went, 'Are your eyes hurting? Because they're killing me.'"

"Coming from me, it's not a line," he said. "It's the truth."

"Lindsay, I think you'd like this mask."

I jerked to the side, and there was Ryan, dangling a mask in front of my face.

"What's wrong with the one I have on?" I asked.

"Probably nothing, but this one is a better quality. Try it on. You'll see." He turned to Jake. "I know you need to make sure everyone is getting what they need. I'm familiar with snorkeling. I'll help Lindsay get her equipment."

Jake grinned at him. "Thanks." He touched my shoulder and winked. "I'll check in with you later."

As soon as he walked away, I jerked off my mask and glared at Ryan. "What do you think you're doing?"

"Saving you from a land shark."

Oh, I wanted to screech!

"Are you crazy? He's a nice guy who's giving me a little attention. Not that it's any of your business."

"You're right. You're right. Your love life is none of my business. But I do know snorkeling equipment." He held up the mask again. "Humor me. Try it on."

I snatched it away from him and put it on. Then wished I hadn't, because he was right. It felt more comfortable than the one I had on before.

"Okay, with your hand, push it against your face," Ryan instructed me.

I did.

"Now, inhale through your nose."

"I don't have the snorkel," I told him.

"I know. What you want to do is create a vacuum. When you move your hand away, if the mask stays against your face, it's a good fit. Try it."

I took a deep breath through my nose, felt the mask suction against my face, and moved my hand. It stayed put.

"Shake your head," he ordered me.

I shook my head back and forth, nodded up and down. The mask stayed in place.

Ryan grinned. "Good."

I took it off:

"See? Jake running a finger around your face doesn't tell you a damn thing," he said.

I narrowed my eyes at him. "I'm sure we would have gotten around to doing the breathing test if you hadn't interrupted."

"I'll just bet." He took the mask from me. "The one you were trying on at first didn't have this purge valve." He pointed beneath the nosepiece. "Sometimes no matter how well the mask fits, you'll get water up inside the mask. You press on this valve, and it removes the water so you don't have to lift the mask away from your face."

"You think I should have that?" I asked.

"Yeah. It's a nice feature. Come on. I'll help you get your snorkel and your flippers."

I had to admit that Ryan did seem to know his way around the equipment.

When everyone had their equipment Jake gathered us around, and we headed toward the beach. Once we were at the edge of the water, Jake had us all sit. He explained everything we had to do. I listened to every word, memorizing all that I could.

I was amazed by all the little things he explained that had never occurred to me: how to pressurize our ears, that objects in the water were actually smaller than they appeared.

"The exact opposite of that sideview mirror on your car that warns you things are closer than they appear," Jake said. "In the water they're smaller."

"So what looks to be a thirty-two foot white shark might only be thirty feet?" Ryan asked. He was sitting beside me.

Jake grinned. "That's right."

"Are there sharks out there?" Brooke asked, clearly alarmed.

Jake grimaced. "I won't say that you won't see any, but they aren't common. I doubt you'll see any great whites. If you see any sharks at all, it'll probably be a nurse shark." He shook his head. "It won't bother you. These creatures see a lot of humans, but they'll still be wary of you. You'll mostly see stingrays, some very colorful fishes, some unusual crabs.

"Any questions?" Jake asked after he was finished telling us how to go about getting into the water, and what to watch out for.

He grinned. "All right then. I want everyone to count off."

We were sitting in a haphazard line, but we managed to count off. I was number four.

"Okay, dudes," Jake said. "If you called out an odd number, look to your left. Even numbers look to your right."

Jake's instructions had me looking at Ryan, Ryan looking at me.

"You're looking at your partner for the day," Jake said.

I shouldn't have been surprised, but I was. Somehow Ryan always managed to be the one who I was supposed to do things with. On the other hand, since he was experienced, if I left him for a while to spend a little time with Jake, it might be all right.

"Put your flippers on," Jake ordered. "Now stand up and turn around. We want to walk slowly back into the water until it's at your waist."

Glancing over my shoulder, walking backward in flippers was awkward, to say the least. I could hear a few people laughing. I was afraid to lose my concentration on where I was going though, afraid I'd trip. I wasn't exactly the most graceful creature as I flopped across the sand in my flippers to the water's edge. And I certainly did feel like a creature. One from the Black Lagoon.

"This is weird," I said.

Ryan took my hand. "Sometimes it helps to hold on to someone," he said. "For balance."

That sounded like a come-on line if I ever heard one, but I had to admit that it did seem to make the going easier as we backed into the water.

The water was so clear. Like glass. Really amazing.

I was so accustomed to the brown water off the coast of Texas that this Caribbean water still amazed me with its clarity. I mean, really, weren't these the same waters that stretched up into the Gulf of Mexico, and eventually lapped at our shores?

How could it be so different here? And yet it was.

We stopped when the water reached our waist. I could see the white sand beneath the water, my flippered feet, and a few tiny creatures moving about.

"Okay, spit into your masks," Jake said.

"Ew!" Brooke called out beside me. "How gross is that?"

"It's either spit or fog up," Ryan said.

"I'd rather fog up," Brooke said.

I spit onto my mask and wiped my spit around the glass. The concept was a little gross, but I'd seen Richard Dreyfus do it in *Jaws*. Following Ryan's example I rinsed my mask with a little seawater, and then I put it on and placed the snorkel in my mouth.

I remembered Jake's instructions to begin breathing through the snorkel.

"Remember if you go under the water, the snorkel closes up," Ryan said. "Don't panic. You're not going to breathe in water, and you're not going to drown."

I bent slightly and squatted until my face was in the water. I put one hand on the sand to balance myself, and then extended my legs back until I was floating. Then I kicked a little.

I was snorkeling!

I had to admit that I felt a little claustrophobic, and it took me awhile to trust myself to breathe through the snorkel without having a feeling of panic.

But the world beneath the water was incredible. So many colorful sea creatures swam around us. I knew we weren't supposed to pet them, but it was so tempting. Touching them could remove their protective layer, causing them to get an infection. I thought it would be a real shame for any of this to be destroyed.

I felt a nudge on my shoulder and looked over. Ryan was signaling down. I searched in the direction he was pointing.

A stingray glided through the water. I knew stingrays were abundant in this area because they'd learned that people would feed them. But actually watching them floating around us . . . oh, gosh, it was awesome. It was like being inside a huge aquarium, only it was all natural. It was nature. And it was unbelievable.

Ryan did some more pointing, and then I watched as he dove beneath the surface of the water. We were still in fairly shallow waters, but it was safe to dive.

I'd listened intently while Jake had given us

instructions on how to dive. So I took a deep breath, ducked my head, and fluttered my feet. Down I went.

Ryan was so right to suggest that I purchase the equipment, because I was hooked. As a matter of fact I was giving thought to looking into some serious diving.

I caught up with Ryan. He pointed out various things until I couldn't hold my breath any longer. I kicked to the surface, inhaled deeply, and relaxed as I waited for my heartbeat to slow.

I thought I could stay here forever.

"That was totally awesome!" Brooke said. "Did you see the octopus?"

We were sitting on our towels on the beach, chilling out after our snorkeling expedition. The guys were around us, sipping their beers, while Brooke and I were drinking water.

"I didn't see the octopus," I told her, "but I saw a tiny shark."

"I saw mermaids," Chad said with a sly grin.

Brooke leaned over, and slapped him teasingly on the arm. "You did not."

"You girls should have gone topless," Cameron said.

"Brooke did," Chad remarked.

My mouth dropped open as I looked at Brooke. With a shrug, she adjusted her floppy hat. "Just for a little while. I wanted to shock the fish."

"Shocked me," Chad said.

I glanced over at Ryan. He was keeping awfully quiet, and I had a feeling he might have caught sight of Brooke with her top off as well.

Part of me wished I'd been that bold. But swimming topless in the Caribbean hadn't been on my to do list. I hadn't even contemplated the notion.

"Hey, Lindsay, why didn't you take your top off?" Cameron asked.

"I'd be afraid a fish would come up and nibble on me," I admitted.

"It's not the fish nibbling that you'd have to worry about," Chad said.

I felt my face grow hot with embarrassment. I definitely hadn't figure out a flirtation style that wouldn't get me into trouble.

"Okay. You guys who are renting, if you'll give me your equipment, I'll go turn them in for you," Jake said.

He started gathering things up, and looked

over at me with a wink. "Lindsay, would you mind helping me?"

I felt Ryan's, as well as Brooke's, gaze fall on me. I decided to ignore them both. "Sure."

I helped collect the equipment, then followed him back to the diving shop so it could all be returned.

"How'd you like snorkeling?" he asked.

"Loved it," I said. "I think I'd like to do some scuba diving."

"You could take a class on Cozumel, get in a little shallow diving maybe."

"I might do that."

"Are you sure there's nothing between you and Ryan?" he asked.

"I'm sure."

"It's just that he seems to really keep an eye on you."

"Friend of the family. That's all." Calling Ryan a friend of the family was becoming second nature.

We walked into the shop and returned all the equipment. When we stepped back outside, Jake took my hand and led me around to the side of the building.

"I'm new to the ship," he said. "I was wondering if you could give me directions to your cabin."

Before I could comment, he kissed me.

It was a breath stealer. Probably the best kiss I ever had. When we broke apart, I was panting a little.

Jake tucked a strand of hair behind my ear and grinned. "You know I shouldn't have done that, right?"

I nodded.

"So let's keep it our little secret."

"Sure."

He sighed with obvious regret. "We need to get back to the others."

I followed him around to the front of the building. We both came to an abrupt stop. Ryan was standing there, feet spread, arms crossed over his chest.

"How would you like to go to Hell?" he asked.

CHAPTER 24

Like so many tourists, we all went to Hell simply so we could say we'd been.

Although I wasn't a hundred percent sure that Ryan's question had been completely in reference to the small town in the Cayman Islands. A part of me thought that maybe he'd been issuing a threat.

Jake certainly hadn't seemed to take it that way though. He'd rounded everyone up, put us on a bus, and took us to Hell.

Hell was located on the north end of the island. It got its name from the unusual jagged, black rock formations that looked like the charred remains of a hellfire, but were actually a type of limestone coated with algae.

Along with other tourists, we stood on a boardwalk taking pictures of the formations. Then we had our pictures taken with a one-dimensional wooden cutout of the devil, dressed in red with a pitchfork and pointed tail. We shopped for T-shirts at the Devil's Den. Naturally

I bought a postcard to send to Julie. I wrote a quick note on the back, "Wish you were here in Hell with me!"

I bought a stamp, and dropped it in the mailbox along with about a thousand other postcards that would be sent from Hell.

That night, after we'd all cleaned up and gotten the sand and surf off, we met up at Cruisin'. It was way different this time than it had been that first night. It was like we were all connected, and it was hard to believe that we'd only known one another for only a few days, a few nights. It was like we were all becoming friends. Real friends.

We'd kinda confiscated one section of the club, pulled tables together, and ordered a pitcher of strawberry margaritas. Ryan was at the far end of the table, talking with Cathy. As a matter of fact the guys had situated themselves so each one of them was sitting beside one girl. I wasn't sure how they'd managed to do it, but it was like they were settling in, realizing some of them might have a chance of hooking up with one of us before the cruise was over, while the others were destined to simply be along for the fun.

Marc sat on one side of me, Michael on the

other. Brooke was splitting her time between Marc and Shooter.

"You know," Brooke began, "we can say we've been to Hell and back."

"That's exactly what the T-shirt I bought says," Shooter announced. "'I've been to Hell and back.'"

"Dog, today was awesome," Marc said. "I think it was the best so far."

"I'll drink to that," Shooter announced. We all drank to it. Several times in fact. We ordered another pitcher of strawberry margaritas. I was feeling really relaxed and totally happy.

"Wanna dance?" Marc asked me.

"Sure."

We headed to the dance area. I was feeling so good, and I knew that the margaritas weren't totally responsible for my attitude. Although I still had items on my list that I hadn't yet checked off, I was having a great time on this vacation. I'd met some fun people, experienced some new things.

And as I danced with Marc, I was beginning to think that I might have even figured out the flirtation game. Several guys had shown an interest in me. I still hadn't found the guy who would be my last night fling. But I was more comfortable with looking.

When the music ended, Marc and I walked back to the table. An order of nachos had arrived with the new pitcher of drinks.

I dropped into the chair and reached for a cheese-laden chip. "I'm starving. Whose idea were these?"

"Ryan's," Shooter said. "Not only that, he's picking up the whole tab. Everybody's drinks. He told us to order whatever we wanted."

I glanced down the table at him. He was leaning forward, grinning and talking with Donna now.

"Is he, like, rich?" Brooke asked.

"I don't think so." I wondered if Walter had given him permission to charge things as well.

"We've had a lot to drink tonight," Brooke said. "It's going to be an expensive tab."

"Don't worry about it. If he says he can pay for it, I'm sure he can pay for it."

She leaned across the table toward me. "Why don't you think he's hot?"

"I do. He doesn't think I'm hot."

"That's bull. You're the reason he hangs around with us."

I shook my head. "He's like all of us. He doesn't want to be on this cruise alone. That's why he joins us."

"I don't think it's *us* at all," she said. "I think it's only *you*. I think you're crazy to be sitting down at this end of the table."

"Hey, if he was interested in me, he could come down here."

"Maybe he feels like he's been rejected too many times. Guys have really sensitive egos. Tell them no once and they're, like, bruised forever. Girls heal. We're tough. We bend. Guys break."

"Who made you the new Dr. Phil?"

She nudged Shooter out of his chair, and scrambled over so she was sitting beside me.

"'Girls on cruises who can't get laid.' That would be a great show, wouldn't it?" she asked.

"You've hooked up with at least half these guys," I reminded her.

"And not one has made me forget about Chris. Isn't that a bitch? I need to find someone who will hang around for more than one night." Reaching across the table, she grabbed the pitcher and refilled her margarita glass and mine.

"Drink up, Lindsay. It's the easiest way to forget that we don't have anyone special."

"Brooke, you are a total downer, you know that? I'm having a great time. Or at least I was until you got all morbid on me."

"I'm trying to have a good time, Lindsay. It's just not working. I miss having one guy."

"Stop comparing them all to Chris. Find someone totally opposite who doesn't remind you of him."

"Totally opposite? That's a thought." Suddenly she perked up, and smiled brightly.

I figured she'd determine who would be the right guy for her.

Then I felt a warm hand on my shoulder and heard a familiar voice. "Hey, can I join you guys?"

I glanced up and there was Jake.

"Sure," I said with a smile. I looked at Brooke, and signaled for her to move over.

Jake sat in the chair beside me.

"So are you off the clock?" I asked.

"Unfortunately, no, although it's really fortunate."

"That's confusing. How can it be both?"

"Well, if I was off the clock, I'd have to be belowdecks. We're not allowed to fraternize up here. Since I'm on the clock, I thought I'd check

252

on my favorite group of singles."

"We're your favorite group?" Shooter asked.

"You bet," Jake said. "We'll be in Cozumel tomorrow. I've chartered a bus so we can go see some Mayan ruins. How does that sound?"

"Sounds cool," Brooke said.

"They're neat to see," Jake said. He leaned closer to me. "And people will have a chance to go off by themselves. I won't have to watch everyone so closely." He lowered his voice. "They won't have to watch me."

He leaned even closer to me, and lowered his voice even further. "Thought maybe we could have a picnic. We could discuss the possibilities in about an hour . . . in your cabin?"

CHAPTER 25

I was pacing in my cabin, trying not to be nervous. Trying not to read more into Jake's comment than he'd meant.

After I'd whispered my cabin number into his ear, he'd grinned and winked at me. Then he'd stood up, announced that he'd see everyone at nine in the morning, and left.

I'd checked my watch, finished my margarita, danced with Marc again, declared myself wiped out from such a busy day, and returned to my cabin.

I was light-headed from the margaritas, and really wishing that I hadn't had quite as many to drink. The temptation to simply lie down and take a quick nap was so great.

I dabbed my special love potion perfume that I'd bought in St. Thomas behind my ears, on my wrists, and at the hollow of my throat. I brushed my teeth and gargled.

I turned down the bedspread, decided that was too blatant an invitation, and remade the bed.

He was coming to discuss a picnic. What was there to say about a picnic? Discuss the food? Exactly where to have it? What kind of blanket to sit on?

I tightened my hands into fists, and tried not to get too excited. But it was almost impossible. This could be it. This could really be it.

Jake and I had clicked from the beginning. He was cute. There was a romantic aspect to getting involved with a crew member. Didn't it happen in the movies all the time?

I knew Jake probably wasn't supposed to take an interest in the passengers, but when you were soul mates—

The phone rang, nearly giving me a heart attack. I snatched it up. "Hello?"

"Hi, Lindsay, it's Mom."

I sat on the bed, wishing I hadn't picked up the phone, but I'd thought maybe it was Jake. "Mom. Hi."

"I haven't heard from you so I thought I'd check in. You're hard to find, though. You never seem to be in your cabin."

"I'm usually out having fun, Mom."

"I'm glad to hear it. What have you done?"

I rolled my eyes. Her timing couldn't have

been worse. I really wanted to be psyching myself up for Jake's arrival. Still, I couldn't be rude to my mom. "I've snorkeled and shopped and parasailed . . . so many things, Mom. And I have pictures so I can show them all to you when we get home."

"Did you want to try to meet up tomorrow—"

"I'd love to Mom, but a group of us have already made plans to go to the Mayan ruins."

"That sounds like fun. I'm glad you've found some friends to hang around with."

A light tapping on the door made me jump as much as a loud bonging would have. "As a matter of fact, Mom, someone is here now so I need to go."

"Okay. Tell Ryan that we say hi. Walter is having a hard time getting in touch with him as well."

"We're having fun, Mom. I'll check in with you later."

After I hung up, I rushed across the room, and opened the door.

I couldn't stop myself from smiling at Jake. "Hi."

"Hey." He slipped inside and quickly closed the door. "Didn't want anyone to see me or to get the wrong impression."

"Right. I'm sorry I had to keep you waiting. My mom picked the wrong time to call."

"Is she on the cruise?" he asked.

"Yeah."

He glanced around the room. "She's not going to show up here, is she?"

I laughed lightly. "No. She's on her honeymoon. I have this room to myself. Did you want something from the minibar?"

"Yeah, a beer would be nice."

"Okay, sure. Yeah."

I couldn't believe how nervous I was. I had all the lights off except for the lamp by the bed. And it was turned on its lowest wattage. I'd wanted a romantic feel to the room.

I took a beer out of the fridge and handed it to Jake. I wiped my hands on the sundress I was wearing.

"You changed clothes," Jake said.

I nodded. "Yeah. I just . . . I don't know. I just thought I should."

He set the beer aside without even opening it.

"You're nervous," he said quietly.

"I've never had a guy in my cabin before," I confessed.

"You can't tell anyone that I was here."

"Oh, I won't," I promised.

"There's all these rules," he said. "No one really pays any attention to them. We all break them. As long as we're not caught . . ."

"I understand," I assured him.

He stepped toward me and took my hands. "It's really hard when I see a beautiful woman, and I know she's untouchable."

I felt the heat burn my face. "I'm not untouchable."

He grinned. "I'm glad."

He kissed me, and I decided that my flirtation skills had definitely improved.

The kiss was hot and slow. It left no doubt in my mind what he wanted, and where this kiss would lead.

A loud knocking had us both jumping apart.

I laughed self-consciously, embarrassed to have reacted as though a gun had gone off in the room.

"I think someone was knocking down the hallway," I said.

He furrowed his brow. "Didn't sound like it was down the hallway. Sounded like it was for here."

"That's impossible."

But the knock came again, and darn it, it did sound exactly like it was—

I spun around. Ryan was standing on my balcony, pressed up against the glass door.

"What the hell?" I muttered.

I charged across the room and pulled open the door. "What are you doing? How did you get on my balcony?"

"I climbed over from mine. I didn't figure Casanova here would let you open the door to the hallway."

He strode into my room as though I'd invited him or worse yet, as though he owned it.

"Hey, Ryan," Jake said. "This isn't what it looks like."

Ryan crossed his arms over his chest. "What exactly *is* it, Jake?"

"None of your business is what it is," I said, letting my anger fly. I couldn't believe that he was here, ruining my perfect night.

"Look, Lindsay—"

"I know Walter wanted you to look after me, but I'm not a child. I can make my own decisions."

"Walter?" Jake asked.

"And your own mistakes," Ryan said.

"This isn't a mistake," I retorted.

"No? Do you know where he was this afternoon when we were snorkeling? He didn't stay in the water with us. And he didn't leave the water alone."

I felt as though he'd slapped me. "You don't know what you're talking about."

"Don't I?" He gave Jake a hard glare. "Tell her, Jake, or I will. Tell her who you were with. You know how I know who he was with? Because I just spent thirty minutes consoling her while she cried."

He'd been talking with Donna the last time I'd noticed him. Donna who'd been on the excursion with us. I turned to Jake. "Jake?"

"Who's Walter?" he asked.

"My stepdad."

"Not Walter Hunt," he said.

I nodded. "Yeah. So?"

"Shit." He turned as pale as the underside of a stingray. He looked at Ryan and held out his hands. "I can explain."

I stared at him, feeling a roiling in my stomach. "Ryan's telling me the truth. You were with someone this afternoon?"

"It's a party cruise," Jake said. "I hang out

with singles. Why do you think they're here? Come on. We all want to have a good time."

Yes, I'd wanted a good time, I'd wanted to have a fling, but somehow I'd expected more of a commitment from the guy. I didn't want to be like Brooke, trying every guy out. I wanted one guy who thought I was special. I thought I was going to bring up the nacho I'd eaten.

"I think you should leave," I said.

"Look, Lindsay, I thought you were looking for a happening time. It would have been good; fun. You know, a few laughs. Some good times."

"Just leave."

He took a step back. "You won't say anything to Mr. Hunt, will you?"

"No! I won't say anything to anyone." I was majorly embarrassed, mortified. I didn't want anyone to know how stupid I'd been. It was bad enough that Ryan was going to know.

Jake shifted his gaze to Ryan. "It's all about good times, man. You can understand that."

"I understand that when we dock tomorrow, you better resign, walk off the ship, and not walk back on it. Or I will tell Mr. Hunt."

If looks could kill, I thought the glare Jake gave Ryan could have stopped his heart.

Jake spun on his heel, jerked open the door, and stalked out.

I dropped down onto the edge of my bed. "You're not really going to tell Walter, are you?"

"If I see Jake on this ship tomorrow evening, I will. Walter doesn't need a gigolo on his cruise ship."

My head came up. "Walter owns this cruise ship?"

"Yeah. Why do you think that we're going on a route that's so different from the ones most of the cruise lines take? Walter customized it for his honeymoon, and extended a special offer to the public. No sense in taking the ship out if you have empty rooms."

I buried my face in my hands, not really caring about Walter, or his cruise ship, or the route we were taking. All I cared about was that I'd met a guy who'd turned out to be Mr. Wrong.

"I am so embarrassed. I believed Jake thought I was special."

"You are special." Ryan knelt before me. "Look, Jake's a player. He played you, Donna, and no telling how many other girls on this boat."

I came up off the bed. "We're all players, Ryan."

"Look, Lindsay, I know you want something special to happen on this cruise. But not with a guy like Jake. Any dude at that table tonight would be better than Jake."

"Only none of those guys at that table tonight created sparks like Jake did! You just don't get it. You don't know what I'm looking for or what I want. You keep butting in when it's none of your business."

I spun around, giving him my back. I felt tears stinging my eyes, and I didn't know how much longer I could hold on before breaking down completely. "Will you just leave?"

"Are you going to be okay?"

"No, I'm not going to be okay. I feel used. Okay? Are you happy?"

"Not particularly. But you would have felt more used in the morning when you found out this guy puts notches on his nautical headboard."

"Unless I never found out. Then I would have been happy in my blissful ignorance."

"But you deserve better than that, Lindsay. You deserve better than him."

He left then, and I was alone in a room that seemed suddenly incredibly empty and stank of designer perfume. Oh, gosh, I never wanted to smell this fragrance again. It would always remind me of the night I'd almost been a fool.

Almost been? Who was I kidding? I'd been a fool. Completely.

I went to the bathroom, located the bottle of perfume, tried not to remember how much fun I'd had purchasing it, unscrewed the cap, poured the contents in the toilet and flushed, and dropped the empty bottle in the trash. Probably an overreaction, but I felt like I had to do something.

I caught my reflection in the mirror. With my finger and thumb, I created an L, and pressed it against my forehead.

"Loser!"

I walked back into my bedroom, turned off the lamp, and curled into a ball on the bed.

I started crying. The tears just welled up from deep inside me. I was such an idiot. This whole trip I'd been so worried about losing my virginity. My obsession had tainted everything. I was such an idiot.

Jake would have been exactly what I was looking for. A one-night stand. A perfect one-night stand.

Damn Ryan for being right. I would have hated Jake and myself in the morning. I would have felt empty.

Fun for one night, but when dawn came over the horizon, what would we have had?

Nothing really. Nothing that would have lasted.

I heard a soft knocking on my door. I was going to kill Ryan if he didn't leave me alone.

The knock sounded again.

I forced myself to get out of bed and cross over to the door. I looked out the peephole. It wasn't Ryan.

I opened the door. "Brooke, what are you doing here?"

"Ryan called me. He thought you might need someone to talk to."

I rolled my eyes. "He needs to mind his own business."

"He told me everything. So how are you really?"

"I'll survive."

She held up a white box. On top of it was a brown sack.

"I wasn't sure what your food of choice was when you're depressed so I raided Krispy Kreme and the Häagen Dazs shop."

"Doughnuts *and* ice cream?"

"Yeah, decadent huh? Can I come in?"

I wasn't really in the mood for company, but how could I turn away sympathy food? "Sure."

I stepped back and she came in.

"Should we eat on the deck?" she asked.

"So Ryan can hear us talking? I don't think so."

"Okay, how about here?" She spread a towel on the bed, and put her offerings on it. "Come on."

I sat down, fluffed the pillows behind my back, and pressed up against the headboard. I removed a doughnut from the box. It practically melted in my mouth.

"You know, Lindsay, ninety-nine point nine percent of all guys are jerks. They all just want to get us into bed."

"Supposedly they think about sex, like, once every seven seconds," I told her.

"More like every three seconds. It's the reason it's so hard to have a conversation with guys. They lose their train of thought after three seconds, and they're thinking sex again."

"You know, Brooke, I've been totally insane

worrying about being a virgin. I wanted to have a fling with someone I'd never see again, simply so I could get this being a virgin thing over with."

She opened a small tub of ice cream and dipped in a plastic spoon. "Look, Lindsay, I'm telling you—as a friend who has been there and done that. It's better when the guy is special."

"Was Chris special?" I asked.

"Yeah, he was." She popped a spoonful of ice cream into her mouth. "I sent him a postcard from Hell."

"What did you write on it?"

"Something original: 'Wish you were here.'" She sighed. "The thing is, Lindsay, I really wish he was."

And I wished I could find one guy in this world that I cared about that much.

"I have this stupid list of all the things that I wanted to accomplish while I was on this cruise," I told her. "Want to help me revise it?

She grinned. "Sure!"

x Soak up the rays.
x Shop until I drop.
x Drink margaritas by the pitcher.
x Dance all night.

x Climb a waterfall.

x Snorkel.

      more
x Kiss ~~a lot of~~ cute guys.

x ~~Make love~~

x ~~Sleep with a guy for the first time.~~

FORGET ABOUT A SUMMER FLING. JUST HAVE FUN!

CHAPTER 26

Cozumel Day Seven

The sparkling emerald water of Cozumel was exactly what I needed the next morning. The colorful garland of reefs that surround the island and the brightly colored sea life were a balm to my bruised heart.

The Usual Suspects—as I was beginning to think of our little group—had met up early that morning and voted to do the snorkeling thing right off the bat.

Surprise, surprise when Jake wasn't the one taking the votes. Cindy, the bubbly girl who had helped during my mom's wedding, was going to be our leader today.

It seemed Jake had to resign unexpectedly to take care of his ailing mother. A part of me felt sorry for him. I didn't think he'd really meant any harm. He was, like most of us on the cruise, simply looking for a good time.

But Ryan had a good point. He shouldn't have been doing it while he was working. Work isn't a vacation. Didn't I know that well enough?

269

I tried not to let on how bummed out I was, but I felt as though the bubble had fizzled right out of me. Part of the reason was that I felt like I'd gotten exactly what I deserved.

I'd been completely stupid. As I snorkeled through these amazing waters, I thought about how I should have been paying more attention to what was going on around me, rather than focusing on me and my stupid quest.

Really. Who the hell cared if I was a virgin? No one had ever asked me if I was one. The only one who cared was me, and I was finally realizing that it didn't really matter what my status was. It didn't define me.

Scratching the task off my list last night had been liberating. I didn't have to worry about it anymore. It was no longer an issue. As Brooke had suggested for my final task, I was just going to have fun! This vacation still had the potential to be the very best one I'd ever been on.

Later that afternoon a boat took us to the mainland. Cindy had explained that we were welcome to join her excursion, although everything was fairly easy to find.

The little group that Brooke had assembled over time voted to go off on our own. Then Ryan suggested we do something totally crazy, and we all agreed. Instead of taking a tour bus to the ancient Mayan ruins at Tulum, we decided to rent two-passenger mopeds. Brooke suggested that we partner up as we had the day before when we'd gone snorkeling.

Which left me riding on the back end of a light blue moped with my arms around Ryan.

He hadn't said a single word to me all day. Not even when the gang went snorkeling that morning. He just kept watching me closely as if he thought I might do something rash—like take off my clothes, and run through the streets buck naked while screaming my head off.

But crying my eyes out had taken care of any self-destructive tendencies I might have had. No sense in embarrassing myself further.

The trek to Tulum took us well over an hour. Although the puttering mopeds didn't allow for conversation, they were way more fun than riding on a tour bus.

The Mayan ruins were perched on top of limestone cliffs, protected by the sea on one side and walls on the remaining three.

We parked the mopeds in the parking lot provided, which was a good distance away from the ruins. We could have hopped on a bus, but we decided instead to walk the quarter of a mile or so.

At the entrance, we could have hired a guide, but his promises to show us all the places where virgins were sacrificed wasn't really appealing to me. I really didn't care if I never heard the V-word again.

We entered the ruins through a low tunnel in a crumbling wall, which had once served as a means of defense.

Once we emerged into the ruins, the sites were something to behold. Huge stone structures that an ancient civilization had built greeted us.

"Man, I figured looking through old ruins would take about five minutes," Shooter said. "Looks like it might take all afternoon."

"We're not on any schedule," Ryan said. "Other than getting the mopeds back before dark. Anyone can leave whenever they want."

Brooke came up to me, and put her arm around me. "Are you going to be okay?"

"Sure. Look, nobody died okay? I'm totally cool."

"All right then. I'm going to hang out with Shooter. We might not stay all day."

"Like Ryan said, that's the beauty of the mopeds. We can pretty much leave when we want."

"Okay. Have fun."

Everyone else began wandering toward the ruins, leaving me and Ryan standing there awkwardly. I knew I needed to do something, say something—

"The Temple of the Descending God is supposed to have an awesome view from the top," Ryan said quietly, as though he was afraid a loud noise might do some damage to either the ruins or me.

"I'm not going to shatter," I told him.

He looked down at the ground. Then back up at me. "I got to thinking about what you said. And you were right. It was none of my business." He shook his head. "Charging over the balcony like the caped crusader . . ."

"Look, it's over and it's done, and I know you meant well, so let's just enjoy the rest of this vacation, okay?"

"Okay."

I shifted my backpack on my shoulders. For today's excursion, we'd all brought backpacks with water, snacks, and anything else we thought we might need to get us through the afternoon.

We weren't allowed to climb or enter most of the structures. I thought the Castillo—the Castle—was the most impressive structure from the outside. It was my vision of a Mayan temple.

Right beside it was the Temple of the Descending God. We were allowed to climb its stairs, and Ryan was right: The view of the ocean from here was awesome. The blue waters just stretched out forever.

"Can you imagine being the first explorers to discover this place?" Ryan asked.

"I wonder what happened to the people who first lived here."

"No one really knows. It's one of the mysteries of the world. Where did the Mayans go?"

Tourists were swarming over the place, so we didn't stay up there looking down for long. We visited other structures. I couldn't explain what was appealing about looking at the rocks and stones. You'd think if you saw one ancient ruin you'd seen them all.

But there was something mesmerizing about each one.

Away from the main ruins, we ran across the

altars. Although we hadn't hired a guide, one was there with another tour group. He was explaining the ritual virgin sacrifices made here.

I couldn't seem to escape it.

"I think he's just entertaining them," Ryan said. "I don't think virgins were really sacrificed here."

"There is a bit of irony in the possibility, though, isn't there?"

Before he could answer I turned to walk back toward the Castle.

"Hey!" It was Brooke waving her arm and hurrying toward us.

"We found a break in the cliffs. We can get down to the beach. Come and join us."

The cove was made up of fine sand. The water of the Caribbean lapping at the shore was calming. I took my towel out of my backpack and spread it on the sand. Then I laid down beside Brooke.

Ryan and Shooter waded out into the ocean.

"I heard one of the guides say that they sacrificed virgins," Brooke said.

"I heard the same thing. I don't believe it."

"I would think the practice would lead to a promiscuous society."

"Definitely. I can't see that being a virgin would have had any kind of advantage."

"So did you and Ryan make up?"

I turned my head and looked at her. "There was no making up to do. We're buds. That's all."

"Lindsay, I think you're blind."

"Oh, and you have twenty-twenty vision? Shooter is guy number what of how many?"

"Exactly," she said. "My experience is what makes me so keenly aware of the attraction between people."

I laughed and closed my eyes. Brooke was as lost in her own world as I was in mine.

"It would never work between Ryan and me," I said speculatively.

"Why not?"

"Because he's Walter's godson, and there's that whole trusted-friend-of-the-family thing . . . and if we hooked up and then broke up, there would be that whole awkwardness at family and friend get-togethers. And it's going to be awkward enough as it is. Plus we'll be going to the same school for a couple of years, so that's another opportunity for our paths to cross when we might prefer that they not."

"So, don't break up."

"Like you can control *that*."

"Not everyone has as broken a track record as I do. Sometimes things do work out for people."

"Sometimes," I murmured.

"Are you ready to finish touring the ruins?"

I opened my eyes. Ryan was standing over me.

"Sure."

He extended his hand. I grabbed it, and he pulled me to my feet. I packed up my sandy towel and, with Ryan beside me, headed back toward the ruins.

I couldn't seem to wrap my head around this whole concept of finding the right guy. Maybe it was more like knowing you'd found the right guy when you found him. I'd thought Jake was the right guy—and he'd turned out to be so totally wrong.

I was still stinging from that realization.

Distracted, not paying attention as we trudged back to the ruins, I looked to the side as an iguana caught my attention. I placed my foot where it shouldn't have been or on something it shouldn't have been on. I wasn't sure.

I just knew that it twisted oddly, and pain

shot through my ankle.

"Oh!"

I dropped to the ground and bit back a curse. Ryan knelt beside me.

"What happened?"

"I don't know. I wasn't looking where I was walking."

"Let me see."

"I'm sure it's all right. Just help me up."

But it wasn't all right. Pain ricocheted through my ankle whenever I tried to put weight on my foot.

"Oh, great!" I muttered. "This is just great."

"What happened?" Brooke asked as she and Shooter hurried up the path.

"She twisted her ankle," Ryan said. "I'll carry you to the moped, and take you back to the ship."

"You're not going to carry me."

"Sure I am. You can ride on my back. Won't be hard. I hike all the time carrying weighty backpacks."

Terribly offended by being compared to a "weighty backpack," I hopped on my one good foot and hit his shoulder. "I'm not weighty."

"Prove it," he said.

He turned his back to me. "Come on. Get on."

With Shooter's help I managed to do just that—climb onto Ryan's back. He hooked his arms beneath my legs, and supported me while I wound my arms around his neck.

As he trudged up the trail, I wondered if this vacation could get any worse.

CHAPTER 27

It *could* get worse. Or at least that's what I was thinking as I sat up in my bed with my foot elevated and ice packs around my ankle.

It had been near sunset when we'd finally been able to get back to the ship, with me hopping on one foot from place to place—whenever Ryan wasn't carting me around like an overloaded backpack.

The ship's doctor diagnosed my injury as a "slightly sprained" ankle. He'd wrapped it, and told me to keep it elevated and on ice for the evening.

Here we were in Cozumel, where the nightlife was really something we could all get into, and I was stuck in my cabin. The others were on the island, probably eating at Hard Rock Café or Planet Hollywood. After which they'd hit the discos.

We weren't leaving until tomorrow afternoon, and here I was, my last night in this port, totally and completely alone.

I'd forbidden Ryan to tell Mom that I'd hurt myself. No reason to ruin her honeymoon simply because I'd ruined my vacation.

Ryan had gotten a key to my cabin—"So I can check on you without you having to come to the door."

He'd brought me to my room, using a stupid wheelchair that the doctor had provided. He'd helped me onto the bed.

The first thing he'd done was put the remote control within my reach. So typical of a guy to think my main concern was not being able to access television.

Then he'd made ice packs, and wrapped them around my ankle.

He'd actually been very nice, and I did appreciate all that he'd done. He'd made sure that I had something to drink and snack on. He'd been the perfect nurse.

And then he'd left.

From my bed I'd watched the sunset through the doors leading out to my balcony. Alone. I did not want to spend the last night in this port having a one-person pity party.

I thought I heard a commotion in the hallway, and then there was a knock on my door.

"Lindsay, it's Ryan. Can I come in?"

I was never in my entire life so grateful to hear his voice.

"Yes! Come on in."

Hurry, hurry, hurry. I would be grateful for any company. I heard the keycard click, the handle turn down . . .

The door opened and the Usual Suspects poured into my cabin. Brooke led the way.

"Since you couldn't come to Cozumel for the night, we've brought Cozumel nightlife to you," she announced.

I felt tears sting my eyes. It was the pain medication I'd taken. It made me all weepy.

"Oh, guys, you didn't have to do that."

"We know," Shooter said. "But what are friends for?"

And I realized that they were my friends. That during this week, we'd developed a bond. It had kind of snuck up on me, but it was there.

Someone plugged in a portable CD player with speakers, and music was filling the room. Pizza boxes were spread out on the coffee table. An ice chest was placed near the bed.

Cameron opened it. Inside were iced-down bottles of beer, and two pitchers of frozen margaritas, one of which was strawberry.

"Oh, guys, thanks, but I took some pain meds and I can't have alcohol."

"Not a problem," Brooke said. "Ryan told us that would be the case so . . ." She lifted out the strawberry pitcher. "This one's a virgin."

I laughed. How typical.

"And we can raid your minibar to make individual non-virgin drinks," Brooke said.

"Make yourselves at home!" I exclaimed.

And they did.

My cabin, because it was so large with a sitting area and the balcony, was perfect for a party. People gathered in little two- or three-people clusters on the balcony, in the sitting area, and on my bed.

The people on my bed constantly changed, as though I were a queen and they were subjects coming to visit. I was surprised by how much we had to talk about.

We'd so moved beyond that first awkward, "Where are you from?"

The cruise was winding down, and it was like we were just gearing up.

The one person who didn't come to talk to me, the one person who seemed to stay at the edge of the party, was Ryan. More an observer than a participant.

Around two o'clock, Brooke announced that it was time for this party to end.

"I'll check in with you tomorrow," she said. "We're going to get up early in the morning, and do a little scuba diving before the ship leaves port."

"Oh, that'll be fun. Don't worry about checking on me, though. Just get to the beach as early as you can."

"You sure?"

"I'm sure."

"We'll miss you."

One by one, everyone stopped by and said good-bye: Marc, Shooter, Chad, Cameron, David, Michael, Cathy, and Donna. We'd all become quite the group.

When everyone had left, Ryan began gathering up the empty pizza boxes and the discarded beer cans.

"Leave all that," I said. "The maid can clean it up in the morning. I'll give her a really nice tip."

"It'll just take me a second. I even came prepared." He dug a plastic bag out of his jeans pocket, and shook it open. Then he began dumping all the trash into it.

"Was having the party your idea?" I asked.

"Brooke and I sorta hatched it together."

"So I guess you don't see her as a trouble-causing octopus anymore."

He grinned at me. "She has her good points."

He closed up the bag, tossed it toward the door, and walked to the bed.

"You need anything before I go?" he asked.

What I needed was for him to stay, to sleep with me like he had that first night, curled around me. But I couldn't tell him that. Instead I just shook my head.

He shoved his hands into the back hip pockets of his jeans. "Listen, I thought if you were feeling up to it, we could rent a couple of horses tomorrow. Take a quick tour of the island. Riding a horse wouldn't put much pressure on that ankle."

"Ryan, that's nice of you to offer, but you should go scuba diving with the others."

"I've scuba dived before. I'd just as soon tour the land as the sea."

"Are you sure?"

"Absolutely."

"Okay, then, yeah, I'd like to go horseback riding tomorrow."

"Great."

He walked to the head of the bed, leaned down, and brushed a quick kiss across my lips. "See you in the morning. Call me if you need me before then."

He turned and headed for the door.

"Ryan?"

He stopped and looked over his shoulder at me.

I swallowed hard. "Thanks . . . for everything."

"Anytime."

He picked up the trash bag and left.

And I found myself wishing so badly that he'd stayed.

CHAPTER 28

There was something old-fashioned and leisurely about riding horseback through a lush tropical forest.

Ryan and I were in a group of six. A guide led the way.

My ankle was feeling much better. We'd stopped by the onboard medical station before we left the ship, and the doctor put a brace on my foot. I tried to keep all the pressure off my ankle, but I was beginning to see why he'd diagnosed my injury as slightly sprained.

I suppose if it was badly sprained, I would have spent another day bored, in bed, with my foot elevated.

Instead I was out in the heat and the humidity. The guide had told us that we'd be traveling through a Mayan jungle, but it wasn't exactly what I'd call a jungle. Jungle brings up images of Tarzan.

We were traipsing through what I would call a forest.

The paths were often narrow, and Ryan had to follow me. Whenever the paths widened, he'd come up beside me.

We didn't do much talking. Mostly we just listened to the sounds of the forest, caught sight of a few animals, birds, and butterflies.

When we came out of the forest, we rode down to the ocean. We dismounted, and our guides removed our saddles so we could ride bareback through the surf.

It was something I'd always thought would be a romantic thing to do. I had to keep my foot up so the brace didn't get wet, but there was something special about riding along the beach. The clear water lapping against the horses' legs.

I thought about my new friends and wondered where they were off diving. If they'd explored sunken ships or discovered buried treasure.

And I thought about Ryan, giving up the opportunity to join them for something that was interesting, but hardly exciting.

He pulled his horse up to mine.

"Well, it isn't exactly scuba diving," he said.

"I was sorta thinking the same thing. Are you too terribly bored?"

"Not at all. How's your ankle?"

"It's feeling better. I feel so stupid—"

"You shouldn't."

I shook my head. "I can't believe you're hanging out with me when you could be having such a good time with all the other people we've met. I think Walter owes you another cruise."

"You think I'm here with you because of Walter?" he asked.

"Well, yeah. He asked you to look after me—"

"And you told me that you didn't want to be looked after."

I shook my head. "Then I don't get it, Ryan. Why are you here?"

"Because I want to be."

Because he wanted to be.

I sat in a lounge chair on my balcony, gazing out at the quickly darkening sky, thinking about Ryan's words. In typical Lindsay Darnell style, I hadn't known what to say, how to respond.

Because part of me was afraid to read too much into his words. To hope that he'd grown to like me as much as I'd come to like him. Ryan who knew about my stupid list and hadn't tried to take advantage of it. Ryan who always seemed to be there right when I needed him.

Except tonight.

I figured he was out with the gang. Brooke had stopped by to let me know that everyone was going to fill up on margaritas at Cruisin' tonight. And that she'd see me tomorrow.

I didn't blame them. The gang had been great to come party with me last night, but I couldn't expect them to do that again tonight. Everyone was here to create memories.

The ship had left port near twilight. Tomorrow we'd be in Cancun. I'd decided that if I rested my ankle one more night, tomorrow I should be able to hit the beach for some sun and fun.

I heard the sliding of a glass door, and glanced over toward Ryan's balcony. He stepped out of his room.

Wow, did he look hot tonight. He wasn't dressed up. Just wearing a black T-shirt and jeans. But it was obvious that he was freshly showered and shaved. Hair was perfect. Everything was perfect.

He did that familiar hitching up of a corner of his mouth, and my stomach knotted up like it always did. It occurred to me that maybe I should have blown off my search for the perfect guy to sleep with and simply spent more time with Ryan—even if only as a friend.

Brooke had been fun, no doubt about it. But I also really enjoyed Ryan's company. For the first time in my life, I thought maybe I finally understood that old saying about not seeing the forest for the trees.

I'd been so busy searching for Mr. Perfect that I might have missed my opportunity to hang around with Mr. Fun-and-Sexy. And our paths were bound to cross in the future since he was sorta family. And we would have had great memories to fondly talk about. I was beginning to think I'd really blown it.

"I knocked on your door," he said.

"I didn't hear it."

"How's your ankle?"

I shrugged. "I still can't dance on it."

He grinned. "So what's the problem? You couldn't dance before."

I stuck my tongue out at him. "I dance great for your information."

"You sure did at the wedding reception. Want some company?"

Did I ever. But it was unfair to him . . .

"My party isn't nearly as fun as the ones

taking place on other parts of the ship."

"But it could be."

He held up a bottle of champagne and two flute glasses. I wondered if the champagne was the bottle he'd snitched the first night. Suddenly he was climbing over the railing that separated our balconies.

"Ryan!"

With a grin, he settled into the chair beside my lounger. "It was quicker than walking around."

"You're crazy," I told him.

"Crazy about you."

My heart thudded against my chest, and Ryan looked out toward the horizon as though embarrassed by what he'd said.

I told myself that it was just a comeback line, didn't mean anything. I mean the truth was in his actions. His actions.

While everyone else was off partying, he was here on my balcony.

Bringing the party to me last night.

Carrying me from the Aztec ruins.

Saving me from a smooth-talker.

Snorkeling with me.

Tossing me into the pool at Dunn's River Falls.

A movie . . .

The list seemed to go on and on. There was that missing the forest for the trees thing again. I'd been so busy looking for someone to have a fling with that I hadn't noticed what was right in front of me.

A friend. If not a lover.

"So what are you going to do tonight?" he finally asked.

"I'm not going to dance. That's for sure. Thought I'd watch the stars come out. Maybe read. Or start planning the rest of my summer."

He glanced over at me and grinned. "You're big into planning, aren't you?"

"Yeah, I like to have goals, I like to know where I'm going. I like to have accomplishments that I can tick off."

"Like sleeping with a guy?"

I shook my head in wonder. "I can't believe I told you about that the first night."

"You were a little tipsy."

"More than a little." I shrugged. "At least I got to check it off."

"You did?"

I nodded. "Yeah, right after that first night when I *slept* with you."

He laughed. "Ah, slept, slept."

"Right. But I've discovered that it shouldn't have been on my list at all," I conceded. "I'm thinking that it should be spontaneous, unplanned. You know why?"

"Why?"

"My list was all the things I wanted to be sure to experience on this cruise. I did almost all of them. I should feel a sense of accomplishment. Right?"

"I'd think so."

I shook my head. "The crazy thing is, for everything on my list that I checked off as accomplished, the things I remember most are all the moments that weren't planned, that weren't on my list."

"Like twisting your ankle?"

"Like having an unexpected party in my cabin."

"You did look like you were having a good time."

"Why aren't you out partying with the others tonight?"

He shrugged. "I'll admit I started connecting with the group at the end, but my main reason for being with them isn't there any longer."

"What was that?"

"You."

"Because you need to keep an eye on me?"

"I told you this afternoon that's not the reason I'm hanging around." He shifted in the chair and faced me. "It bothers you that I'm Walter's godson."

I nodded. "Yeah, it does."

"Why?"

"Because if things don't work out, it would be awkward whenever our paths crossed."

"So it's crossed your mind that there could be something between us."

"Sometimes, I think about it," I admitted. "But I know that you think you have to baby-sit me—"

"Lindsay, I've never baby-sat in my life, and I'm certainly not going to do it on a cruise."

"But you said—"

"So what am I going to do? Tell a chick who's looking for someone to become a check mark on her to do list that I'm hanging around her and her newfound friends because I think she's cute?"

My heart did a hard slam against my ribs.

"You think I'm cute?"

"From the minute I saw you. But I don't

want to be a check mark. Task completed. Move on to the next one."

"It wouldn't have been like that," I said quietly. But I could see where I might have given the impression that it would have been. I shook my head. "But, Ryan, other than when we were parasailing, you've never said or done anything that made me think you were truly interested in me."

"I know. I didn't figure Walter would appreciate the direction my thoughts were going in when it came to his new stepdaughter. He brought me on this cruise to be a traveling buddy, someone to keep you from being alone . . . not someone to get you into the sack."

I found it difficult to breathe.

"So you thought about getting me into the sack?"

"Oh, yeah. Then I'd get so mad because you were throwing yourself at some of these scumbags—"

"I never threw myself at a scumbag! I was experimenting, testing the waters. Looking for Mr. Right."

"And he was right next door, all along."

I scoffed. "Ha! You wish."

"Yeah, I did," he said quietly.

I didn't know what to say. What to do. There was such sincerity in his voice. Such, well, yearning . . . like maybe he really had been hoping all along that I would be to him what I'd been wishing he'd be to me.

He stood. "Well, guess I'll go see what's shaking at the clubs."

Reaching out, I took his hand. "Ryan . . ."

My mind was a jumble of thoughts and emotions. What to say to make him stay? Or should I let him go?

"I didn't think you liked me," I blurted.

"Yeah, well, you were wrong." He pulled me to my foot, my good foot, and wrapped one arm around me, holding me against him so balancing on one leg wasn't such an effort.

And then he kissed me. Tenderly. Warmly.

I felt as though I was soaring, like when we were parasailing, only my feet were on the ground. Or at least my good foot was. The other was raised, like a flamingo.

But I didn't care. I only cared about this kiss that felt so right, so perfect, and that I knew I wanted more than anything in the world—and more than once.

Ryan drew back, then pressed his forehead against mine.

"Tomorrow is our last stop. Cancun. Do you think we might see where things go if I forget that you're Walter's stepdaughter and you forget that I'm his godson?"

"Yeah," I said quietly. "I'd definitely like to see where things go."

CHAPTER 29

Wearing swim trunks and a muscle shirt, Ryan showed up at my door minutes after we docked. I was wearing a spaghetti strap tank and shorts over my bathing suit. I had a canvas tote that carried all my beach essentials, and a netted bag that had my snorkeling equipment in it. Ryan took both from me.

Then he took my hand. I was nervous, excited, scared, and happier than I'd been the entire cruise.

"Where are we meeting Brooke?" he asked.

"We're not. She called this morning, and said she had some other plans. Which works for me."

"Works for me too." He leaned down and kissed me. "So, are you ready?"

Smiling, I nodded. "Definitely."

The white sandy beaches and the blue, blue waters of Cancun were just what the doctor and Cupid ordered. We'd spread our beach towels over lounge chairs beneath umbrellas. I set my tote bag nearby. I was wearing a water-repellant wristband with a zippered enclosure inside, which I'd placed anything of real importance: money, the key to my room, my I.D.

"You want to snorkel first?" Ryan asked.

"Sure."

We got ready. Everything seemed so different this time. Before I'd been a novice, learning the ropes. Not that I was totally experienced but I was more familiar with what I was doing. Plus this time I didn't have Jake around to distract me. Or Brooke. Or anyone else.

It was just Ryan and me.

My ankle was feeling much better. I tried not to put too much pressure on it, but I was fairly certain it would be fine in the water.

As soon as we were geared up, Ryan and I headed for the water. I still felt funny walking over the sand with flippers, but I was also excited about exploring the corral reefs and seeing the brightly colored sea creatures.

We got to the water's edge, turned at the same time so we could back our way into the water, and took each other's hand. Only there was another difference this time. We weren't holding hands for balance. We were holding hands because we wanted to be connected.

Once we were snorkeling, gliding through the water, we continued to hold hands. We pointed out various fish and crabs and urchins to each other. It was a more deeply sharing experience than we'd had previously. Although we'd shared the world beneath the sea before, it just had a different feel this time that was difficult to explain.

Everything seemed brighter, more colorful, more alive—as though I was viewing every aspect of this special world differently. I wasn't thinking about my to do list or what I needed to check off.

I was simply enjoying the moment, enjoying being with Ryan. It was so magical, and I was glad that this last day before the ship turned toward home that I had Ryan all to myself.

When we'd seen all we wanted to see, we headed back to shore. As soon as we were out of the water, I sat on the sand and removed my flippers. "That was awesome," I said.

"I never get tired of snorkeling," Ryan said. "It's such a fascinating world."

He stood and helped me get to my feet. "How's your ankle?"

"It just has a little twinge, so I might even be able to dance tonight."

"Great."

We walked back to where our loungers waited. I dropped my gear onto my bag and stretched out on my stomach so the heat, sun, and breeze could dry me off. It felt wonderful.

"Want something to drink?" Ryan asked.

"Yeah, I'll take a margarita."

"I'll be right back."

I reached for my sunglasses, put them on, and watched him jog to the thatch-roofed building, where drinks were being made. "Lindsay Darnell," I murmured, "you were crazy not to have been spending all your cruise with him."

We spent the afternoon lounging in the sun and sipping margaritas. I was feeling terrific. Lying on my back now, I looked over at Ryan and found him watching me.

Smiling, I crooked my finger and wiggled it, signaling for him to join me. With a grin he got up, came over, and stretched out beside me. Although we were on a crowded beach, we weren't the only ones sharing a lounger.

Since we were both wearing bathing suits, it felt really intimate. Ryan lowered his mouth to mine. It was wonderful. Hotter than the sand beneath us.

And I couldn't help but wonder: If this is what the afternoon holds for me, what will the night hold?

The evening was more fun than the afternoon had been. Ryan and I ate dinner at the Hard Rock Café. Drank more margaritas, and talked as much as we could in a place were loud music made it difficult to hear.

"What's college really like?" I asked.

"Some partying, mostly studying," he said.

"I hear the classrooms are big."

"Your core classes are usually held in auditoriums. Upperclassman classes are smaller."

"I'm nervous."

"You'll do great."

I reached across the table and took his hand. I liked being able to do that without worrying about what he thought or if it was the right thing to do.

"Are you ready to head back to the ship?" he asked.

I wasn't . . . and yet I was. It was our last night at a port. In the morning the ship would set sail. We'd spend tomorrow evening on the sea and arrive in Galveston the day after that. It seemed that everything was moving quickly now. Coming to a close.

"I'd like to walk along the beach first," I told him.

"We can manage that."

When we reached the beach, I slipped off my sandals. The sand felt wonderful beneath my soles.

The sun had almost set. The sky and the ocean were beautiful. I felt as though I was in paradise. And then Ryan took me into his arms and I knew that I was.

The kiss was slow. Exploring tongues. As somewhere off in the distance, the sun sank below the horizon. A ship's horn blasted. The roar of the surf filled my ears, or maybe it was simply the rush of my blood.

Our bodies were pressed close. Our mouths closer. I couldn't have placed the kiss into a category if I'd had to. It was too incredible for words.

Ryan drew back slightly, and pressed his forehead to mine, his arms looped around me, his hands resting against the small of my back. My arms were wrapped around his neck.

"So what did you think?" he asked.

"Spectacular."

"The day?"

"You."

"So does that mean that you want to spend tomorrow together as well?"

"Definitely."

CHAPTER 30

The Enchantment **Night Ten**

The last day and night of the cruise were insane, as though everyone onboard could sense the minutes ticking down before the cruise ended. Everyone wanted to cram in one more moment of fun, one more margarita, one more dance, one more kiss.

Our little group had spent much of the day together at the pool and the miniature water park. Riding the waterslides. Playing water volleyball. Soaking up the sun.

The entire time, Ryan was at my side, sneaking in kisses now and then. When we scored in volleyball. When we shared nachos. When we went down a waterslide together.

I suppose it was becoming evident to everyone that we'd hooked up, because none of the other guys were trying to get my attention.

With my back to his chest, his arms around me, I stood on the top deck with Ryan and watched the sun set on our final night of the cruise. Sometime tomorrow we'd arrive in

Galveston. I couldn't believe that I'd been gone for a little more than a week. In a way it seemed like a lifetime.

We weren't the only ones on the deck. It was crowded up here, and I wondered if Mom was up here with Walter. If she was, I didn't see her.

"Do you want to hear something totally crazy?" I asked Ryan.

"Shoot."

"I had all these plans for this to be the very best vacation of my life. Nothing went as I planned. But you know what? I don't think I'd trade a single minute of it. Especially the last two days."

His arms tightened around me. "I'm glad to hear that. And we still have all of tonight. I don't think anyone is planning to sleep."

I certainly wasn't.

When the sky darkened and the stars came out, Ryan and I headed to Cruisin'. We found Brooke sharing a table with our little group. She was sitting between Shooter and Marc. They'd been on either side of her all day. I didn't want to contemplate that maybe she was planning to spend her last evening with two guys. But if she was, that was totally her business. Not mine.

Although we ordered pitchers of margarita, I only drank one glass. I didn't want to lose sight of my last night, to get wasted, or to even have a buzz going. I didn't mind the one drink to relax me, but I wanted to make memories tonight. And margaritas were more for those who might be wanting to forget things.

I didn't want to forget a single moment of this last night of the cruise. Ryan and I were together. Snuggled up against each other, talking quietly, kissing occasionally, and dancing when the music suited us.

We were so in tuned. As though we were reading each other's minds, knew what the other was thinking, what the other wanted.

As the night progressed, the party got louder. People got drunk. Chad passed out again. His buddies left him on the floor where he landed.

It was nearly midnight when Ryan said, "I can hardly think in here anymore."

"Me either."

"Want to go?"

I nodded. Then I leaned toward Brooke. "We're going."

"Okay. See you at the pool tomorrow."

I walked out of Cruisin' with Ryan's arm

around me. We walked to the elevator. No one else was inside. When the doors closed, he took me into his arms and kissed me. Hungrily, greedily, as though he couldn't get enough of me.

Which was fine with me. I couldn't get enough of him either.

"So you wanna check off that last task?" he asked.

"No."

His head came up, and I could see the confusion in his eyes. He obviously thought I was rejecting him.

"I want to make love with you, though."

He furrowed his brow. "I don't understand."

"Neither did I. Not at first. I thought it was all about losing my virginity. And that's really, so totally, not even an issue. I just want to be with you. Virgin or not."

A slow grin spread across his face. "Let's make it not."

The elevator stopped on our deck. We got off. With our arms around each other, stopping every few feet for a kiss, we finally made it to the door to my room. I reached into my purse, pulled out my key, and handed it to him.

With a grin he slipped it into his pocket, and

tugged me to his room. Inside he had chilled champagne waiting.

He poured us each a glass.

"What if I'd said no?" I asked.

"I would have gotten drunk." He tapped his glass against mine. "Here's to ending this cruise the way you planned."

But when we set our glasses aside and fell onto the bed together, I knew we weren't going to end this cruise the way I'd planned.

Because I'd never planned to fall in love.

CHAPTER 31

The next morning I went down to the pool. Brooke was already there, lying on a lounger in our favorite area.

I dropped down on the deck chair beside hers. "So how are you this morning?" I asked.

"In love."

I felt my eyes widen. "With whom?"

She blushed. "Shooter."

"You're kidding."

Grinning she shook her head. "I'm so stupid, Lindsay. I was so caught up with sleeping with every guy around that I totally missed the boat. So to speak. He's everything Chris isn't. And get this." She leaned over and grabbed my arm. "He's not upset that I slept with all his friends. As long as I don't do it again."

"So you're going to keep seeing him?"

She nodded enthusiastically. "Can you believe it? I feel like such an idiot. He was there all along, and I just, like, so did not see him. Which is quite a feat considering how tall he is."

311

"I don't believe this!"

"I'm having a hard time believing it too. I'm just so happy. And Chris. I hope he gets my post-card, and I hope he does go to hell."

I laughed. This was unbelievable.

"What about you?" she asked.

"What about me?"

She angled her head as though she wanted to study me. "Do I look stupid? I saw the way you and Ryan were looking at each other last night, and kissing every chance you got."

I felt the heat rush to my face. "We had our own little private party after we left Cruisin'."

She squealed and squeezed my hand. So un-Brooke-like.

"I knew it. From the moment he brought you your earring. I knew he was your destiny."

"We'll be at the same university in the fall, so it'll work out."

"This is so totally cool. Who would have thought we'd both fall in love on this cruise?"

"It was definitely the very best vacation I've ever had."

"We'll be docking in Galveston this evening," she said. "Want to grab our guys and do a little partying?"

"Can you party with just four people?" I teased.

"Definitely. How about you?"

"When one of them is Ryan, I can party with just two."

"Speaking of . . ." She nodded in the direction behind me.

I turned and there was Ryan, striding toward me. I'd certainly seen him looking happier—especially last night.

"Hey, Brooke," he said without smiling.

"Hey. Think I hear Shooter calling for me. See you when we dock."

She walked off.

"Why are you going to see her when we dock?" Ryan asked.

"We're going to party in Galveston with her and Shooter."

"Shooter? She's with Shooter?"

"Looks to be serious."

"Man, I never would have figured that match up." He sat on the edge of my lounger. "Do you have something against waking me up in the morning before you leave?"

I sat up and pressed a kiss to his lips. "You were just sleeping so soundly that I didn't want to disturb you."

He grinned. "So next time, disturb me."

"What makes you think there'll be a next time?" I teased, knowing without a doubt that there would be.

"Because I love you."

I wound my arms around his neck. "That works for me."

"Yeah?"

"Yeah. Because I love you too."

Then he gave me one of those soul-searing, heart-stopping kisses that I'd discovered he was very good at.

I'd cruised the Caribbean. But Ryan was taking me places that I'd never gone to before.

Being with Ryan wasn't about a task on my to do list.

Being with Ryan was simply about . . . being with Ryan.

From *Spanish Holiday* by Kate Cann

Oh, God, he's pawing at her face again. Oh, God, stop him. If he does that thing he does—where he paddles his fingers down her face and grabs hold of her cheeks and squidges her mouth up . . . I'm going to kill him. I'm going to have to.

I watch helplessly as Tom squeezes in Ruth's face and makes her mouth look like a duck's bill. I stare as he kisses her, saying, *Ooo-ooh, Roofy-Roofy*. And I don't make a move to even slap him, let alone kill him.

I'm demoralized, that's what I am. Passive, helpless, and demoralized. I've been on this Spanish trip one week three days, and that's approximately one week one day too long.

Tom, Ruth, Yaz, and I are sitting in a fake touristy taverna at a table for four, drinking ready-made sangria and waiting for our sham paella to arrive. Yaz and I are silent, and the canned flamenco music is happily too loud for us to hear what Tom and Ruth are whispering about. Although I can guess. They're kind of gurgling and gnawing at each other across the red-checked tablecloth, and then Tom comes up for air and asks, "Well, I said I'd get us here, didn't I girls, eh?" and Ruth says, "I know, I know, you're *brilliant*, baby."

I try to make sickened eye contact with Yaz but she's staring straight ahead.

"Senor—senoritas—dinner is served!" Two waiters swoop four microwaved plates down in front of us—*crash-crash, crash-crash*. I look at the vicious yellow of the rice, the scattering of what might be seafood, and feel ill.

"Looks good!" announces Tom, as he forks a great slimy mound of it into his face.

"Yeah," agrees Ruth, lovingly. "This place is lovely."

"Although I wouldn't mind a steak, tomorrow. Or a burger or something. I'm getting a bit sick of all this Spanish crap, to be honest."

"This isn't Spanish crap," I snarl. "This is tourist crap. No Spaniard would be caught dead eating this."

"Oh, here we go again," sneers Tom. "Lors the expert on Spain."

"Don't call me *Lors*."

"Just 'cos you got your GCSE in Spanish, it doesn't make you an expert."

"I'm not saying I'm an expert. I'm just saying

2

we should eat somewhere *real* for once, and not go in the most *touristy* place in the town!"

"You need somewhere where they've got the prices up in *English*," says Tom slowly, leaning toward me as though explaining to a backward child. "So they can't rip you off."

"Actually," I snap, "that place we walked by that *I* wanted to go in—that was cheaper. I checked the menu."

"Yeah, yeah. Understood all of it, did you?"

"Most of it. Well—some of it."

"Octopus guts and pig's colon—know the Spanish for that do you? Yum."

Ruth starts giggling as though he's hilarious, and I shoot her a look that says *traitor* and hiss, "It looked good. There were Spanish people in there."

"What's good about that? They eat all kinds of rubbish. Anyway, you should've gone in on your own if you felt that strongly about it."

"Oh, come on, Tom," says Ruth. "We've only just got here. We agreed we'd stick together tonight."

Tom splats a kiss on the side of her head, and says, "Yeah, babes, you're right, we did agree. So shut up moaning, Laura. You were outvoted, okay?"

I glare at Tom, out of words. He smirks, triumphant. Ruth looks pleadingly across the table at me and says, "Oh, come on, let's enjoy the meal, shall we?" And there's the briefest of pauses, then we all start forking up the day-glo paella and shoving it in our mouths.

It started as a joke, Tom getting the casting vote because he owns the car. It was funny about twice, then it got to be really grating. We'd pull up outside some gruesome place offering pizza at the top of the menu, and Tom would say, "Looks okay. Less than a fiver a head." And I (or sometimes Yaz) would say, "Why don't we go on a bit farther, see if there's somewhere more interesting?" And Tom would answer, "Okay—put it to the vote. I say eat here." And Ruth (of course) would echo, "Yes—here looks great." Yaz would usually back me up and want to go on, and Tom would say, "I'm the driver, I get the casting vote."

And he'd park the car.

I'd started to hate that bloody car.

Maybe I hated it because we were stuck in it so long each day, all through the loveliest, warmest part of the day, because Tom had this touring fixation. Maybe I hated it because it guzzled so much of my holiday money in petrol even though (as Tom gloatingly reminded us just about every single time he filled it up) petrol was cheaper here than at home. Or maybe I hated it because the car was the principal reason for us all being here together, and I'd started to *really* hate that.

God, what a mistake it was, agreeing to come.

From *MAINE SQUEEZE* by Catherine Clark

"You're not just going to leave me behind, are you? You're not going to strand me on this island. Are you?"

"Don't make fun of me. Just don't." I looked at my boyfriend, Ben, and raised one eyebrow. "But are you seriously that upset about my being gone for a day?"

"Well, no. But it is kind of lousy," Ben said.

Ben and I had just gone for an early-morning walk so we could have a little time together before I drove my parents to the airport. When they first told me they were leaving the island for the summer, I'd had that exact same reaction, which was why Ben was teasing me about it.

I'd kind of panicked at first. I don't know why. It wasn't like it was a deserted island or that I would be stranded—I lived there year-round. By the way, it's just referred to as "the island," like a lot of islands off the coast of Maine, and I'll keep it that way because (a) I'm too lazy to change everyone's names, and (b) I don't want to incriminate anyone. If you've been there, you

1

might recognize it, but I'm going to keep some things mysterious in that Jessica Fletcher/Cabot Cove/*Murder She Wrote*–reruns kind of way.

Not that there will be any murder in this story. Unless crimes of passion, crimes of the heart, count.

Anyway, my parents would be landing in Frankfurt, Germany, tomorrow, while I'd be showing up for my first day of work at Bobb's Lobster. Something about it didn't seem quite fair.

"When do you think you'll be back tonight?" Ben lingered in the doorway of my house, his hands on my waist.

"Maybe seven? Not too late," I said. I'd drop my parents at the airport in Portland—from there they'd fly to Boston, then overseas—then I'd pick up my friend Erica and drive back.

"I wish I could go with you."

"Would you really want to listen to my parents chanting along to German-language tapes in the car because they haven't quite mastered the language yet?" I asked. Not that they'd gotten the hang of French, Spanish, or Italian, for that matter, but that wouldn't keep them from spending ten weeks in Europe. Nothing would. Not even the prospect of leaving me and Ben alone all summer. (Well, only if *his* parents would leave, too. . . .) I wasn't actually going to be "alone" alone, anyway, because three of my best friends were moving in.

I thought back to the night two months before when my parents told me they were going to Europe for ten weeks. At first I thought we were all going together. I was really excited, but then I realized I was not included, that they'd be sipping wine in the Alps while I schlepped melted butter at sea level.

But I couldn't begrudge them this second honeymoon concept—they deserved it. And did I really want to trek all over the world with my parents? I pictured my dad wearing a pair of lederhosen and doing a jig around a beer hall in Austria, while I cowered in the corner, hoping no one would guess we were related.

Then I pictured me, here, alone in this house. Me and Ben. Alone. It sounded too good to be true. I was afraid that they'd make me stay with my Uncle Frank and Aunt Sue.

Fortunately, my parents suggested my friends move in here, rather than me move in with my aunt and uncle. I'd be eternally grateful for that.

Ben smiled. "You're right. I can probably skip

the German lesson in the car."

"Yeah," I said.

"But it's our first day off from school—and our last day off before we start working full-time. It'd be great if we could just go hang out on the beach or something."

"Tell me about it," I said. "We'll just have to make up for it—we'll find an extra day some-where," I said. "We'll both call in sick or some-thing. Middle of July."

"Okay, it's a plan." Ben nodded. "Maybe we'll be sick for two or three days. No, wait. I don't want to lose my job."

There was a knock on the door. "Colleen?" my mother called.

"Is it time to go?"

"Not yet. But there's something important we have to discuss before we leave."

"What to do when Starsky and Hutch get upset when they realize that you're gone?" I asked, referring to our cats. My dad named them after his favorite old television show.

"No. The house rules," my mother said.

What house rules?

4